Hard JUSTICE

the alpha antihero series

SYBIL BARTEL

Copyright © 2020 by Sybil Bartel

Cover art by: CT Cover Creations, www.ctcovercreations.com
Cover photo by: Wander Aguiar, wanderaguiar.com
Cover Model: Kaz van der Waard
Edited by: Hot Tree Editing, www.hottreeediting.com
Formatting by: Champagne Book Design

All rights reserved. No part of this publication may be reproduced, distributed, or transmitted in any form or by any means, including photocopying, recording, or other electronic or mechanical methods, without the prior written permission of the author, except in the case of brief quotations embodied in critical reviews and certain other noncommercial uses permitted by copyright law.

All characters in this book have no existence outside the imagination of the author and have no relation whatsoever to anyone bearing the same name or names. They are not even distantly inspired by any individual known or unknown to the author, and all incidents are pure invention.

Warning: This book contains offensive language, alpha males and sexual situations. Mature audiences only. 18+

Books by
SYBIL BARTEL

The Alpha Antihero Series
HARD LIMIT
HARD JUSTICE
HARD SIN

The Alpha Bodyguard Series
SCANDALOUS
MERCILESS
RECKLESS
RUTHLESS
FEARLESS
CALLOUS
RELENTLESS
SHAMELESS

The Uncompromising Series
TALON
NEIL
ANDRÉ
BENNETT
CALLAN

The Alpha Escort Series
THRUST
ROUGH
GRIND

The Unchecked Series
IMPOSSIBLE PROMISE
IMPOSSIBLE CHOICE
IMPOSSIBLE END

The Rock Harder Series
NO APOLOGIES

Join Sybil Bartel's Mailing List to get the news first on her upcoming releases, giveaways and exclusive excerpts! You'll also get a FREE book for joining!

Hard JUSTICE

the alpha antihero series

One second.

That was all I needed.

My gun in my hand, my finger on the trigger, I waited.

Yesterday I had been driven by revenge. Yesterday my life had been measured in a single act. Yesterday I did not have the taste of her on my lips. Today was different. I wanted more than justice. I wanted the life I had been robbed of.

Except twelve men with guns drawn were standing between me and her, and I should have been dead already. But they made a crucial mistake. They underestimated my resolve.

I pulled the trigger.

*HARD JUSTICE is the second book in the Alpha Antihero Series, and it is a continuation of Tarquin "Candle" Scott's story.

The Alpha Antihero Series:
HARD LIMIT
HARD JUSTICE
HARD SIN

Dedication

For Mom and Dad

"Candle was earth. Dark and dirty between your hands, he rubbed across your skin and left marks as his scent soaked into you like a memory. You smelled him after every rain, and you felt him every time you fell. He'd cradle you if you needed to lie down in the woods, but he'd never lift you up to touch the stars."

—Kendall, from *ANDRÉ*

Chapter ONE

Tarquin

MY WOMAN'S SMALL HAND GRIPPED MY ARM, AND SHE froze. *"Oh my fucking God."*

I shoved her around the corner of the garage as a dozen motorcycles fanned out on the dirt driveway. "Do not look back. Do not stop. *Run.*" I threw down the backpacks as shouting erupted from the bikers. "I will meet you at the cabin. If I am not there within seven sunsets, I am dead. Sell this and get far away from here." I put my knife, the only thing I had of value, into her hand. "Go."

Her small body shook. "They'll kill you!"

I was out of time. "GO."

I did not look back to see if she listened.

I returned to the open side door of the garage where the dead body lay with the hysterical female still crying over him. Pushing the woman aside, I reached inside the dead man's vest, took his 9mm, and checked the magazine. Sixteen rounds. Shoving my woman's small caliber handgun with only four rounds left into my back waistband, I stood and grabbed the hysterical female around the neck.

The first of the twelve men got off his motorcycle with his gun drawn. He glanced at the body on the ground, then glared at me. "You're dead, motherfucker."

Holding the female in front of me, I pressed the barrel of the 9mm against her temple. "Stand down." If he had had any sense, he would have fired already.

"He shot Rush," the female cried. "He killed him!"

Three more men, all armed, all aiming at me, got off their bikes.

I did not know the first thing about the men standing in front of me, but I did know the men of River Ranch. They would not have let a female human shield stand in their way. I would have been dead already.

I drew only one conclusion.

They wanted the female alive.

"Stand down," I repeated.

"Hell fucking no," the first man ground out. "You stand the fuck down. Let go of Stone Hawkins's old lady."

I knew of the term. The female belonged to someone named Stone.

"Fuck this shit." A fourth man who had gotten off his motorcycle took a cellular phone out and held it to his ear. "I'm calling Hawkins."

I scanned the twelve men.

Four in front on foot, all aiming weapons at me. Four in a second row still on their bikes, guns drawn. Four behind them at the ready on their motorcycles, all facing the entrance of the driveway.

The group had been trained.

I could not shoot all eight before I was either overtaken by the men on the motorcycles or shot myself. My thoughts from yesterday resurfaced. If my woman had been River Ranch, I would have fought to the death for rights to her. Apparently my sentiment was coming to fruition.

"Rush is dead, and some fuck has a gun to your old lady's head," the fourth man said into his phone. "No… hang on." His angry gaze met mine. "You declaring war on us?" he demanded of me.

No other option, I revealed my intent. "War, no. Rights to this female's daughter, yes."

The fourth man shook his head and spoke into the phone. "Says he's not declaring war. Fucker says he's got *rights* to your old lady."

"Not this female," I clarified. "Her daughter."

The female in my grasp thrashed at me and cried out. "He took my baby. He took Shaila!"

I tightened my hold on her but said nothing.

"You hear this shit?" The fourth man's facial expression deepened with hatred. "Yeah. Hold on." Sweeping a finger across his phone, still aiming at me and the female, he walked toward me without fear as he held the cellular phone out. "Stone Hawkins on speaker for you."

"With whom am I speaking?" a commanding but not deep voice asked.

My back stiffened at the proper speak. "Tarquin Scott," I answered as the female struggled for air under my armlock.

"And you are, son?" Stone Hawkins asked calmly.

My jaw clenched. "I am no one's son. Is Shaila your daughter?"

Pause. "Yes." Then, "Do I need to be concerned for her safety?"

"Were you concerned for her safety when the man you call Rush drew his weapon on her?"

Stone chuckled disconcertedly. "I'm going to assume you don't know my daughter very well, Mr. Scott, because that question is laughable. Shaila knows how to take care of herself. She doesn't need a lone wolf to protect her virtue. And that's what you are, aren't you?" he asked with artificial kindness. "A lone wolf? No club at your back? My men indicated that you aren't wearing a cut."

Rage fought for purchase, but I did not have time to entertain it. The longer I stood in this standoff, the worse my odds became. "I know your daughter very well."

"Just let us shoot this motherfucker, Hawkins," the fourth man clipped. "We'll take him out before he even thinks about pulling the trigger."

Ignoring the fourth man's comment, Stone Hawkins casually asked, "Mr. Scott, are you still holding a gun to my wife's head?"

"Yes."

"Stone," the female cried out. "Help me!"

Ignoring his wife, Stone Hawkins again spoke to only me. "Mr. Scott, since you already shot Rush, I'm going to assume you have some familiarity with a gun. But tell me this. Was it a lucky shot? Because Rush served."

I did not know who he had served, nor did I care. "Luck had nothing to do with it. Ask your men to look at his right hand. My first shot was a warning for him not to draw. He did not listen."

Giving a wide berth, the first man circled me to glance at the dead man's hand. "He's telling the truth, Hawkins."

"Let me shoot the motherfucker already," the fourth man clipped.

"Thank you for the information, Viper." Hawkins's voice remained calm. "Oslo, if you shoot Mr. Scott and my wife is harmed, do you know what I will do?"

The fourth man, apparently named Oslo, ground his teeth, but he did not reply. He did not have time to.

Hawkins kept speaking. "I will personally go to your house, and I will take your wife and your daughter, and I will make sure both are well used before I hand them over as the new club whores. The men will have explicit instruction to show no mercy."

"The fuck you will," the man named Oslo growled.

I was not educated, but in a single moment, I suddenly understood two things. The twelve men in front of me were weak. And River Stephens, the man who had raised me, the man I despised, the man who single-handedly presided over and controlled the most violent cult in the world, was a genius.

The men in front of me were weak because they were fearful for their women.

The men at River Ranch had no such affliction.

River Stephens had made sure of that. Forcing the men to mate multiple females nightly, not allowing interaction except for servicing and mating, not allowing personal connections—there were no emotional attachments. Unless a brother decided he wanted to be bonded to a female and endured a beating that was designed to take his life, he was not allowed to keep one woman or form emotional connections.

But this was not the case here.

Not for the man named Oslo. Not for Stone Hawkins.

Their weaknesses were my opening.

I made my move.

"Your daughter is no longer your concern," I told Hawkins. "Consider yourself informed. I claim rights. She belongs to me now." I did not hesitate. I fired three consecutive shots before returning my aim to the female's head.

The three men in front all dropped dead from gunshot wounds to their heads. One of them got off a wild shot first that went over my shoulder. Two of the men in the second row got off their bikes while two ducked. The female started screaming, and the man holding the phone raised his aim toward my head. "You're dead, motherfucker!"

"DO NOT FIRE," Stone yelled though the cellular phone.

Still holding the female, I began to back up. "Hawkins, tell your men to stand down, and your wife will survive."

"*Oslo*," Stone demanded. "Who's down?"

Chest heaving, perspiration showing, Oslo unsteadily pointed his gun at me as he glanced at the bodies. "Viper, Dell, and Patch. All dead," he ground out.

I took in Oslo's distress over his dead brothers. Another weakness.

"Scott," Hawkins's voice boomed with authority before turning suspicious. "Where did you learn to shoot?"

I was not educated by textbooks, but I knew cunning, both by definition and in recognition of its use. Stone Hawkins was no River Stephens if his men were out here without him, but make no mistake, he was of the same cloth.

I did not reveal my upbringing. "I have seventeen more rounds, you have nine more men."

Hawkins chuckled as if his men's lives were of no consequence. "That's quite an ego, son."

"I am not your son." The female was trembling in earnest, and I did not know how much longer her legs would hold. When they gave, I was dead. "If you wish to lose more of your men and your wife, continue this conversation."

"Maybe I'm not looking to lose more club members, but gain one," Hawkins placated, speaking in riddle. "Sounds to me like you need a club at your back... *brother*."

His last word, its tone and use, did not go unnoticed, but I did not take the bait. Using the female as cover, pretending to adjust my grip on her, I took another step back.

Oslo glanced behind him at a man in the far row who was aiming a rifle like a hunter. The man tipped his chin at Oslo.

Oslo looked back at me but spoke to Hawkins. "Boss, Rip has a clean shot."

"If Rip had a clean shot, Rip would've taken the clean shot," Hawkins clipped in irritation.

Out of the corner of my eye, I gauged the distance toward the right side of the building. Two paces.

The man named Rip belligerently spoke up. "I got the shot."

He did not have the shot. I had my knees slightly bent. The female's head was in front of mine. Neither my head, heart, nor femoral arteries were exposed. An arm wound would not kill me immediately. I eyed the distance to my left. Five long paces to that side of the building.

"I'll tell you what, Scott. I'm on my way there right now. I think you and I need to have a conversation in person." Hawkins paused.

Saying nothing, I scanned the faces of nine men unwilling to die for this Stone Hawkins.

"In fact," Hawkins continued, "I think we should discuss how you managed to walk away from River Ranch."

The female gasped, and her legs gave out.

Chapter TWO

Shaila

I DIDN'T RUN.

I may not have been the bravest girl who ever walked the Lord's green earth, but I wasn't stupid, neither.

Twelve against one wasn't no kinda odds, and I wasn't gonna leave Tarquin all by himself to fend off those pathetic excuses for men my daddy called brothers. No way. I'd let Tarquin between my legs, and as far as I was concerned, that made him my man now as much as any piece of legal paper the state could've given me.

And I was gonna protect my man.

Fighting off fear, swiping at the stupid girlie tears on my face, I pushed away any thoughts that Tarquin might get hurt, and I ran a wide arc behind the garage and headed back to the house. I didn't spend my whole life watching my daddy operate without picking up a few pointers.

If there were two things my daddy was good at, it was thinking one step ahead and always having a backup plan.

Well, I had a backup plan too.

Five of 'em, to be exact.

A little winded, a lot sweaty, I skirted the back of the house and went to my bedroom window. Thankful I never bothered setting the latch, I pushed the old wood frame up and grasped the sill. Half hoisting, half shimmying, I scrambled my way up and in.

No grace, I landed chest first on my old bed and it creaked something fierce.

Panicked that the sound may have carried, I froze for three seconds while my heart beat louder than the dang bed. Then that stupid son of a bitch Oslo's voice traveled across the yard as he yelled something about shooting Tarquin.

Spurred into action, I moved.

Careful of all the places I knew the floor squeaked, I grabbed my shotgun and fisted a couple handful of rounds, shoving 'em into my pockets next to the knife Tarquin gave me. Then I went for the kitchen and squatted in front of the cupboard under the sink.

Behind the bleach, right where I'd left 'em, I had my backup plan.

Five Molotov cocktails.

Amazing what you can learn on the internet.

Careful as you please, with my shotgun tucked under my arm, I picked up four of them. My arms full, I tiptoe-ran back to my bedroom and set the glass jars on the sill. "Lord, have mercy," I whispered. "Don't let me drop one."

My backup plan settled on the sill, I grabbed a lighter and climbed on my bed. Putting my twelve gauge through the window first, I shoved one leg, then the other out and over, and I dropped to the ground as I heard more yelling by that imbecile Oslo. Only thing worse than a stupid Oslo was an armed Oslo. But I figured him yelling was a sign Tarquin was still okay.

Tucking my gun up under my arm, I picked the four glass jars up, and making a wide arc of the bikers, I hightailed it to the front yard. Crouched low, keeping to the palmettos and buggy-as-hell scrub brush, I set the first two of the glass jars a few yards back from the bikers, and I was about to set up the second two a few feet away when four shots rang out.

"You're dead, motherfucker!" Oslo yelled as my mama started wailing like a stuck pig.

"DO NOT FIRE." My daddy's voice carried over Mama's screaming.

Lifting my head over a group of palmettos, I risked a peek.

Well, *shit*.

Three rows of four bikers each, all lined up pretty as you please, thinking it made them look intimidating. But every one of them was stupid as all get out. They were too stubborn to realize they'd lined themselves up like sitting ducks for anyone who had a semiautomatic. Not to mention, their line of defense hadn't helped the first row one lick.

Three bikers in the front were dead as doornails.

Viper, Dell and Patch were all on the ground with bullet holes between their eyes. And dead center in the thick of it, holding both the proverbial smoking gun and Mama in front of him like a shield, stood Tarquin.

My man.

Taking a step back, Tarquin spoke up. "Hawkins, tell your men to stand down, and your wife will survive."

I glanced at the three down again.

Holy Ghost Almighty, that boy was a good shot.

Real good.

A lick of fear surged right along with the pride I felt for my new man, but I didn't give one single thought to the jerks lying on the ground. And I knew no Lone Coaster would shoot Mama if they wanted to live to tell about it. I hated all of Daddy's MC club brothers. Every last one of 'em. Not a single honorable one in the lot, which was just how my daddy liked it, but they were loyal to him, and Daddy was protective of Mama, and they knew that.

"*Oslo*," my daddy's voice boomed. "Who's down?"

Sweating like a sinner in church, Oslo aimed at Tarquin with a shaking hand as he held his phone out with the other. "Viper, Dell and Patch. All dead."

Daddy had told me once that Oslo wasn't worth nothing but a live body on days you needed someone holding a gun more than you needed smarts.

"Scott," Daddy's voice boomed through Oslo's phone. "Where did you learn to shoot?"

Oh, no.

No, no, no, I silently chanted. *Do not tell Daddy where you're from, Tarquin. Don't do it.* Daddy would use Tarquin as a pawn in a hot second. I didn't know how, but I knew enough to know my daddy would think someone as rare as Tarquin, who'd escaped from River Ranch, was as good as gold. At a bare minimum, he'd use him as bait to get River Stephens's attention, and nothing good would come from that.

"I have seventeen more rounds, you have nine more men," Tarquin calmly replied.

My admiration of Tarquin grew, but I needed to get him out of the line of fire. It was smart of him to have grabbed Mama. Daddy would never admit he had a soft spot for her, and he protected her, but if it came down to it, I was pretty sure Daddy would sacrifice Mama if it meant getting his hands on someone like Tarquin.

Daddy's voice carried through the cell phone's speaker as he chuckled. It was the kind of chuckle he gave to let you know he had the upper hand. "That's quite an ego, son."

"I am not your son." Tarquin immediately retorted as Mama shook like a leaf in his grasp. "If you wish to lose more of your men and your wife, continue this conversation."

"Maybe I'm not looking to lose more club members, but gain one," Daddy replied in his fake-understanding tone. "Sounds to me like you need a club at your back... *brother*."

Tarquin took another step back.

Oslo glanced behind him at Rip who was standing in the back row with a rifle aimed at Tarquin. "Boss, Rip has a clean shot."

I'd been around death my whole life. I'd seen the worst kinda things grown men could do to each other. For the most part, I'd become immune to it. Sad to say, but truth was never pretty. Except today, standing in thick palmettos with no-see-ums biting my legs like sport, I had to admit, fear licked at my spine.

I didn't want Mama or Tarquin to die.

As much as I hated Mama for going along with Daddy's plan to give me to Rush, I didn't want to see her get shot in the head. And I definitely didn't want to see that same bullet rip through her skull and hit Tarquin.

Thankfully, Daddy spoke up with some common sense. "If Rip had a clean shot, Rip would've taken the clean shot."

Rip threw down ego. "I got the shot."

Tarquin glanced left.

Oh, no, not left, baby. That's too far to get to safety.

"I'll tell you what, Scott," Daddy boomed. "I'm on my way there right now. I think you and I need to have a conversation in person."

Every muscle in my body froze with newfound fear.

"Oh no," I whispered. Daddy coming here would make everything ten times worse.

Saying nothing, Tarquin scanned the bikers.

"In fact," Daddy continued, "I think we should discuss how you managed to walk away from River Ranch."

Mama gasped, and her legs gave out.

Shit. I was out of time.

Lighting the Molotov cocktail in my hand, I threw it as hard and as far as I could. Then I whipped my shotgun around and took aim.

The cocktail exploded on impact, and nine bikers stupidly looked in that direction.

Taking aim, I whispered, "Come on, Tarquin, *run.*"

I pulled the trigger.

Chapter THREE

Tarquin

A SMALL EXPLOSION BEHIND THE MAN WITH THE RIFLE MADE every biker turn to look. I let the female drop to the ground, and a shotgun blast sounded.

Enraged, I ran.

As I cleared the side of the garage, another shotgun blast sounded, along with a second explosion.

I knew who it was.

She did not listen.

She had not run.

Gunfire erupted.

Taking cover behind the garage, I dropped and aimed as Oslo ran toward my position. My shot hit him in the forehead. His body fell to the ground as I set my sights on the second row of bikers. I shot one in the back of the head as another dropped from a shotgun blast to the chest. Engines roared, men yelled, a third explosion erupted.

I aimed at the man with the rifle as he aimed at me.

Wood splintered overhead.

Ducking, I cursed myself for flinching as the man with the rifle gave his bike gas.

Amid bullets pinging off the garage and wild shots being fired in the direction of the shotgun blasts where my woman lay, I used the sights on the 9mm and fired at the back of the man with the rifle as he drove down the driveway.

I missed.

Standing, I stepped out from cover as four bikers spit dirt behind their motorcycles in their retreat.

Taking aim, my jaw clenched, I fired again.

I hit the man with the rifle in the shoulder.

His body jerked, his motorbike dropped, and his brothers swerved around him, never looking back as he went down.

The female still alive and screaming, the scent of gunfire and copper everywhere, the man with the rifle lay on the ground, half trapped under his motorbike. Reaching with his good arm, he palmed a holstered gun.

I shot his hand.

He howled like a wolf.

I shot his exposed leg.

He roared.

I shot his good shoulder.

His scream of pain terminated into silent anguish as his mouth remained open. With crazed eyes, his life blood pumping out, he looked up at me.

"Die." I put a bullet between his eyes.

A shotgun cocked with a reload behind me. "We good?" my woman asked in a pant.

I spun.

The taste of rage in my mouth, fury running through my veins, I grabbed her shotgun from her small hands and threw it on the ground.

"Hey!" she barked indignantly. "What the heck do you think you're—"

Stepping into her, I grabbed her throat. "Do. Not. *Ever.* Defy me again," I warned in a lethal tone.

Shock, then anger twisted her expression. "What did you just say to me?"

I tightened my grip as her eyes widened. "You heard me."

Her foot came up, then slammed back down on top of mine, heel first. "Take that."

Never having been defied by a female before, I was not expecting it.

Pain lanced across my foot, and I let go of her throat.

She kicked me in the shin. "And *that.*" She reared back with her fist. "And *this.*"

Her last verbal warning was her mistake.

I grabbed her wrist and jerked. Her body off-balance, she fell into me. "Do you want to hit me?" I seethed.

"Yes, you big dumb idiot. You should be *thanking* me!" She hit her own chest with her free fist. "I *saved* your stupid butt!"

Nostrils flaring, my cock hardened. "You ignored me," I corrected.

"And what *the hell* were you gonna do?" She yelled the question in my face, as if I were not standing directly in front of her. "Die trying to shoot twelve men all by yourself?" She yanked out of my grasp and threw her hands up as she screamed at me. *"How stupid are you?"* Spinning, she kicked the dead rifleman. "You're a stupid jerk too! I'm done with *all* of you!" She bent to reach for her shotgun.

I grabbed her from behind and gripped a handful of her hair.

Letting out an inhuman roar of rage, she kicked out.

The female on the ground in a heap sobbed louder.

I yanked my woman's hair until her head hit my shoulder, then I glared down at her. "Finished?"

Her chest heaving as dead bodies lay all around us, she spat vile words at me. "Screw you."

My nostrils flared. "Speak to me like that again, and I will bend you over and fuck you right here in front of your mother."

"You sick son of a bitch," she growled like a man. "What the hell is wrong with you?"

Arousal warring with anger in my blood, what the hell was right with me? "When I tell you to do something, you do it."

Her mother wailed like a wounded animal. *"Shaila."*

"Oh, yeah?" she challenged, ignoring the female. "To what end, big man? You wanted me to run off like a scared cat, leaving you to die? Get shot all to hell by twelve bikers with even less sense than you? Is that it?"

"Yes," I ground out, gripping her hair tighter. "If that was what was meant to be, then so be it." I would have died protecting her. "But I will not die in vain." Not for a woman who did not respect me. "Do not disobey me again."

"Let *go of me.*" Her elbow reared back, and she hit me in my still bruised ribs.

Taking it like a man, I did not flinch. "You are going to have to work harder than that to injure me." The brothers at

River Ranch had given me a far worse beating, and I was still standing.

With her hair locked in my grip and fire in her eyes, anguish contorted her features. "That's the point, you stupid man! Can't you see that?" Her voice broke, and she stomped her foot. "I didn't want you injured!"

For one heartbeat, the world stilled.

Our gazes locked, our breath in sync, there was no distance between us.

Then my pulse pounded, my life's blood roared in my veins and I did not hold back. I slammed my mouth over hers.

She gasped, and I drove my tongue in.

Growling into my mouth, she both fought against my dominance and fell into me.

I kissed her harder.

Her growl turned into a moan, and the fight left her body.

I stroked my tongue around hers one more time, then reluctantly retreated. "It is time to go. They will be back."

Anguish etched across her face, she looked up at me. "I didn't want you to die."

"Do not put yourself in harm's way for me." I did not understand it, it contradicted everything I had been taught growing up, but I would die for her. Having her put herself in the line of fire, for any reason, only enraged me.

Her voice went quieter. "I was trying to help."

"*Shaila*," the female whimpered.

"I can take care of myself." I released her. "We need to go."

"*Shaila*," the female called again.

Turning toward the woman who birthed her but making no move to go to her, my woman took a deep breath. "I should help her."

The female was strung out like the women on compound who were addicted to the forbidden herb that River Stephens grew deep in the Glades.

I picked up my woman's shotgun. "She was no such help to you."

My woman shook her head as her hands went to her hips. "Yeah, I know."

"We are out of time." I could hear motorbikes in the distance. "How much ammunition do you have for this?" I handed her the twelve gauge.

She took the shotgun like a man who knew how to use it would. Grabbing the stock single-handed, she confidently swung the barrel over her shoulder in one smooth motion as if she had done it every day of her life. "Two, three boxes inside."

"Go get them. I will retrieve the backpacks." I moved toward the female who was still carrying on.

My woman glanced at the bodies in the dirt. "We just gonna… what?" Her arm swept out in an arc. "Leave all this here?"

"Yes." I took the weeping female by the arm and pulled her to her feet before letting go to glance at her frail body. I saw no injuries. "Stop crying."

She wept louder.

"Mama," my woman scolded, as if speaking to a child. "For Christ's sake, cut it out." Taking her arm, she steered the female toward the house. "You've seen way worse than this, so quit your snivelin'. Go inside and smoke some of your weed. Calm down. Do what you gotta do. Daddy'll be here soon. You can save the tears for him." She pushed her up the porch steps and started to turn away.

The female reached for her. "Wa-wa-wait. Where are you going?"

"Away, Mama."

"No! You ca-can't. I need you," the female cried, grasping my woman's free arm with both hands.

Shaila looked at me with exasperation. "She's gonna keep this up."

I listened to the sound of motorbikes in the distance for a moment. They did not seem to be getting closer yet. I looked back at my woman. "Take her inside and get the ammo. Make haste."

Chapter Four

Tarquin

I retrieved the backpacks and was collecting guns from the dead bikers when my woman came out of the house wearing a black jacket and dark glasses pushed to the top of her head.

Carrying three boxes of ammo, her shotgun was over her shoulder. "I told Mama we were heading northeast to Kentucky and to not tell Daddy, no matter what. Which guarantees it'll be the first thing she tells him. So we better get."

Kentucky.

I vaguely remembered the word. Another state.

"All right." I checked the magazine on the last handgun I retrieved. Half loaded. I made a quick visual survey of the bodies to make sure I did not leave any firearms.

"Well, don't just stand there. Help me get this beast up."

I glanced at her as she gripped the handlebars of the motorbike that had belonged to the man Rush. Having been knocked over in the other bikers' hurried retreat, it was now lying on its side.

"What are you intending to do with it?" We did not have time for this.

Standing upright, her shotgun and the extra shells at her feet, she looked up at me as if I had lost my mind. "We ain't just leaving all of 'em. Do you know what one of these is worth?"

She was the one who had lost her mind. I said nothing.

Her eyebrows drew together. "This is a *Harley*."

I did not know the significance of what she was implying. "We are out of time."

Her eyes widened. "What's gonna buy us time better than a Hog?"

Swine would not help us now. "I do not know."

Her hands went to her hips. "Jesus, Mary and Joseph, are you for real right now?" She did not wait for me to answer her question. "This is our ticket out of here. Don't just stand there. Help me get the bike upright."

Understanding took. "You are intending for us to ride that."

"Well, Rush sure as heck don't need it no more, and I ain't stupid enough to look a gift horse in the mouth. And I'm *definitely* not stupid enough to take one of the Lone Coasters' bikes, even if they ain't gonna need them ever again. As far as Daddy'd be concerned, stealin' from a club member would be like stealin' from him, and we're not goin' there. We're already in enough trouble, so no sense addin' to it."

A gift horse? "You cannot drive that to the cabin." There were no roads beyond her property, and the only paths I had ever seen were deer trails. Even a three-wheeled vehicle would have trouble navigating over and through the thick palmettos, slash pines and mangroves.

"Maybe not," she agreed. "But we're not leavin' somethin' this valuable here. So unless you wanna be standing here arguin' about it when Daddy shows up to skin your hide before sellin' you to the highest bidder, then you better unstick your stuck butt and get into gear to help me."

I did not know what I was more appalled by, her manner of speech or her sentiment. Not that it mattered, because there was one critical problem. "I do not know how to drive the motorbike. I have never driven any vehicle."

Her hands dropped to her sides, and she went perfectly still.

She stared at me.

Then her chest moved with a sharp inhale and she blinked. "Okay. Well, first off, it's a motorcycle, not a motorbike. Second, you don't need to know how to drive a Harley. Not just yet anyway. I'll get us outta here, but I can't do that with this beast lying useless on its side. So, chop-chop, lend a hand. Let's get her up and see if she starts." She clapped her hands twice.

"You know how to drive this?" No female on compound knew how to drive a vehicle, let alone a two-wheeled one. It had been strictly forbidden. In fact, only certain brothers with special privileges were allowed to operate the few vehicles we did have at River Ranch.

She scoffed. "I'm Stone Hawkins's daughter. I knew how to ride before my feet could reach the gears."

The sound of motorbikes came closer.

"Come on, come on," she clipped, looking down the

driveway. "We got a better chance on this beast than on foot. I can take us around the back way, and we can hit the cabin from the north. Besides, we need to ride off so Mama tells Daddy we went to Kentucky." She grabbed the handlebars again.

I glanced down the driveway.

I had not thought of the merits of misleading them as to our location. On compound, we had always stayed and held perimeter. We were all taught the dishonor of saving your life over sacrificing it to protect the borders of the compound.

But I was not on compound anymore, and I had more to protect than a chain-link fence.

Shoving the guns into one of the backpacks, then dropping it, I stepped next to my woman. "Move."

Complying, she retreated from the motorbike and picked up the backpack.

I grasped one side of the handlebars and placed my other hand on the frame of the motorbike under the seat. Then I shoved with all of my strength.

I got the heavy piece of machinery upright, and my woman made a whooping sound.

"Yes!" She clapped once, and before I could get the kickstand down, she toed it with her foot and moved in front of me. With the backpack on her shoulder, she grabbed the handlebars and pressed a button on the right. "Come on, come on, start." She pressed a second button on the right handlebar.

The motorbike roared to life.

"*Heck yes.*" My woman revved the engine and spoke

over the noise. "Grab the other backpack and put it in the saddle bags." She shoved her backpack in the bag on the far side of the motorbike then glanced at a lit-up display between the handlebars. "We got over half a tank of gas. We're good to go."

Picking up the second backpack, her shotgun and the ammo, I placed everything except one of the handguns inside the opposite leather bag attached to the rear of the motorbike. Leaving the barrel of the shotgun sticking out from the corner of the saddle bag, I secured it shut and shoved the handgun in my back waistband.

My woman straddled the motorbike. Nodding over her shoulder, she revved the engine. "Foot pegs are on either side. Get on."

I hesitated.

No female had ever told me what to do.

"I know what I'm doing, I promise," she reassured. "All you gotta do is lean when I lean and hold on to me. Come on, swing your leg over and get on."

I took no issue with stealing the dead man's property, even though coveting anything on compound growing up was strictly prohibited, and stealing was a sin punishable by death. Not that there had ever been opportunity or material items worth taking when ownership of anything did not exist.

I was at peace with taking the motorbike and weapons.

I was not at peace with getting behind my woman.

She looked nervously down the driveway. "Tarq, we gotta go."

Tarq.

The shortened version of my name, getting behind her, none of this was sitting right with me, but I could not deny the sound of motorbikes getting closer.

Resigned, I threw a leg over and found one foot peg, but I did not lift my second leg off the ground. "You are going to balance the motorbike?"

She patted my leg like a child. "Gotcha covered. Put your arms around my waist and hang on."

My jaw tight, I put my arms around her and lifted my second foot to the peg.

Pulling her dark glasses down over her face, she simultaneously gave the engine gas and lifted her foot off the ground.

The motorbike shot forward.

My arms instinctually tightened around her waist.

"Don't worry," she said over her shoulder. "I got us."

The engine whined higher, and she pulled a lever with her left hand as her left foot lifted a lever. The engine's whine decreased, and we took on speed until the engine was whining a higher-pitched noise again. Then she repeated the motion with her left hand and left foot, pulling a hand lever and lifting a foot lever, then giving the motorbike more gas.

"What are you doing?" I demanded.

Humid air hitting our faces, the smells of flora and fauna coming at us faster than I had ever experienced, she raised her voice over the wind and turned the handlebars to follow the curve in the dirt road. "Gettin' us outta here."

Both of our bodies leaned the same direction the bike turned and alarm hit. I looked at the ground speeding by. "We will fall." Gravity would prevail.

"No, we won't. I got this." She righted the motorbike after the turn and took on more speed. A lot more speed.

Then something happened.

I was not thinking about River Ranch.

I was not looking for other bikers with guns.

I was not navigating a world I did not understand.

No misunderstood manner of speech.

No men hunting me.

No boundaries.

No woman occupying my thoughts.

Wind.

Earth.

Air.

For the first time in my existence, I understood the word freedom.

Chapter FIVE

Shaila

His arms tightened like a noose around my waist as I took a turn. "We will fall."

"No, we won't. I got this." I came out of the turn, and we were at the end of the driveway. Glancing left and right for the other Lone Coasters or Daddy's SUV, I didn't spot any of them, but I wasn't taking no chances. Instead of turning onto the state road, I drove straight across. The dirt lane continued in a mess of backroads that bordered other parcels of land, but eventually it came out on a county road I could take. A long loop would get us to the back side of Daddy's property, and we could hide the bike somewhere there.

Rush's Street Glide and his stupid custom pipes were so dang loud, I wanted to get as far away from the house as fast as possible. Once we crossed the county road, the dirt lane was no better than Daddy's potholed driveway, but I didn't care. The bike was new and big, and I knew it could handle it.

I opened it up.

Tarquin's arms around me, his body stiff behind mine, we flew down the dirt road.

The air cooled, and the old orchards on either side were alive with citrus blooms. If it weren't for the fact that we were on a stolen Hog with dead men left behind lying on Daddy's driveway, it would've been a perfect moment.

A perfect moment with a grown man who'd never ridden on a bike, or in any vehicle for that matter.

I almost couldn't wrap my head around that. Daddy had taken me on his bike since I was little, and by the time I was twelve, he'd taught me how to ride. He'd always said girls should be on the back of a bike with their old man, but since I was his daughter, I was the exception. He said I needed to know how to handle a bike better than any man in his club.

So he'd taught me.

I used to cherish those memories of Daddy spending time with me, showing me how to shift and turn and maneuver around cones he'd set up in the driveway.

Now all of it was tainted with the fact that he was gonna sell me off like some piece of property with no value except what he could get outta the deal.

Anger surged.

Then, as if he knew what I was thinking, Tarquin's right hand left my waist and his hand covered mine.

He gave the Harley more gas.

I couldn't help it. I smiled like a schoolgirl. "Why, Tarquin Scott, I do believe you've got some biker in you."

His lips touched my ear. "I am nothing like those men."

My smile faded. "No, you sure ain't." For one, he could shoot like the devil himself.

He changed the subject. "What are you doing with your left foot?"

I loved his voice, but I loved it even more on a Harley. "Shifting. There are six gears. First gear you push down, then gears second through six you lift up. Reverse for downshifting."

"And with your left hand?"

"That's the clutch. You need it to shift. Every time you switch gears, you pull the clutch, shift, then give it gas nice and steady as you release the clutch."

"You do not release the clutch all at once. Why?"

Despite us running for our lives, in that moment, I felt lighthearted. "No, I don't. If I did, I'd be jerking us around on this bike like a carnival ride."

"I do not know what a carnival ride is." His hand over mine, he twisted the throttle with a gentleness he reserved for when he was touching my body. "This makes it go faster."

The way he had no inhibitions about life—not with sex, not with asking questions, not with admitting to things he didn't know—my infatuation with him grew. "Yep, that's the throttle." I eased off the gas and pulled the brake. "This hand brake is for the front wheel, and my right foot does the brakes on the rear wheel." I slowed us down and downshifted. "Every time you slow down or speed up, you gotta shift the engine. You hear the engine sputtering when your speed decreases, you know it's time to downshift. You hear a high-pitched whine like the engine's running too hard, then you shift to a higher gear."

"How do you keep the motorbike upright?"

I saw an in. "I'll tell you, but only if you say motorcycle. Or Hog or Harley."

His mouth brushed my ear again, and he pulled the throttle. "How do you keep the motorcycle upright?"

This boy had the devil inside him as sure as Daddy had club life running through his veins, and damn if that didn't make me smile. "I don't keep the bike upright. Speed does that for me."

"And when you turn?"

I didn't know whether to be sad he knew so little about life or be thankful he wanted to learn. "It's simple physics. Forward momentum. You keep the bike movin', and you're good to go. You don't wanna ever slow down too much durin' a turn unless you absolutely have to. And if that happens, put your foot out, hovering over the ground, in case you need it for balance."

"What else?" he demanded.

The impromptu driving lesson taking my mind off how mad Daddy was gonna be, I glanced at the controls. "Right here you got the headlights for driving at night." I turned them on, then off. "Here's the horn, but I ain't using it right now. Only use it if someone's about to run into you." I put the left, then the right, turn signals on. "These are the blinkers. You have to use them every time you turn on a public road to signal which way you're goin'. It's the law."

"Whose law?"

Sweet Jesus, what had I gotten myself into? "Uncle Sam."

"I do not have an uncle."

"Sayin' Uncle Sam is just a way to refer to the US government. They got all kinds of laws and rules. It's why we got police and lawyers and courts. But I digress. There're rules for drivin'. You can't just do whatcha want. You gotta stay within posted speed limits, use a turn signal when you turn, stop at stop signs, let pedestrians go first, and since this is America, we drive on the right. There's also a ton of smaller rules, but those are the basics."

"How do you know the speed limit?"

"There'll be a sign with a number on it." I nodded at the speedometer. "You keep the number on there the same as the speed limit. Well, that is if you don't wanna break the law and get in trouble."

"What kind of trouble?"

"Dependin' on how much over the speed limit, you could just pay a fine, or you could go to jail."

"What is a pedestrian?"

"Another way of sayin' on foot. It's someone walkin'. You always gotta let them go first, especially if you come to a crosswalk." Before he could ask, I explained. "A crosswalk is white painted stripes in the street, usually at the intersection of two streets. It's where people on foot are supposed to walk when they cross the street so they don't get hit by a car."

"You cannot cross streets wherever you chose?"

"Not busy streets with lots of traffic."

He was quiet then for a bit.

I couldn't begin to imagine being him. Knowing life one way your whole upbringing, then all of a sudden being thrown into a world so different, you had to learn everything all at once. I had nothing but sympathy for his situation, and here I'd thrown him in even deeper, getting him mixed up with Daddy and the Lone Coasters and my problem with Rush.

Guilt filled my heart. "I'm sorry I put you in this situation."

"What situation?"

"With me." I steered around a pothole. "With my daddy's motorcycle club. With Rush."

"You put me nowhere. I am here by choice. I could have walked away as soon as I was strong enough."

Shifting, giving the bike more speed, I bit my lip. "Could you have?" I asked, feeling even more guilty. "Where would you have gone?"

"I do not need you."

The words hurt. *A lot.* But I had to remember who I was talking to. "I'm guessing you don't mean that sentiment as anything except pure fact."

"How else would I intend it?"

In all my life, I'd never met anyone even close to as honest as him. "With ill intention, like you were bein' mean. Say we were in a fight and you said, 'I don't need you,' out of spite, just to be mean."

"We are in no such fight, and I would not say words with the sole intent of spite."

Always a little nervous around him, jittery-like, but also feeling the irony of his pure honesty, I smiled. "No, I don't think you would."

"I told you I would not."

And that was it. His word was his bible. I may not have known Tarquin Scott very well, but to the bottom of my soul, deep where thoughts went to hide, I knew that. He was a man with integrity like no one I had ever met.

Chapter Six

Tarquin

I watched everything she did and catalogued it.

Gas, clutch, shift, release, more gas.

Brake, hand and foot, clutch, shift, gas.

Turn, lean, gas, straighten.

Left hand, right hand, left foot, right foot, they all worked together at once.

Like shooting a handgun.

Hands aiming, feet bracing, eyes sighting—it was a coordinated effort.

I took in the machine between my woman's legs and made a decision.

"Stop," I demanded.

Obeying me, she pulled the clutch in, downshifted three times and took her hand off the throttle before squeezing the hand brake and pressing the foot brake in tandem.

The motorbike coasted to a smooth stop.

"What's wrong?" Glancing around, she put both feet down and held the bike upright between her thighs.

"Dismount," I ordered.

Leaning away, she looked over her shoulder at me. Her expression was that of someone fighting amusement. "This ain't a horse. You can just say, get off."

"Get off." My gaze trained studiously on the controls, I did not look at her.

"You thinkin' you want a go at driving this beast? Because I gotta say, while I admire your gumption, this is a helluva bike to get your feet wet on."

I frowned as I looked at letters and numbers I could not read. "My feet will stay dry unless it rains."

"Lord, give me strength," she muttered, pushing her sunglasses to the top of her head. "You sure about this?"

I did not hesitate. "Yes."

She pressed a button on the right handlebar, and the engine shut off. "Suit yourself." She put the kickstand down and swung her leg over. "You ever ridden a bicycle?"

"There were no bicycles on compound." I was not ignorant to the tyrant ways of River Stephens. He had forbidden any vehicles except his few personal motor vehicles. Anything with wheels would have been a means for the brothers or sisters to get away.

"Right." Her hands went to her hips. "Okay. So, here's the deal. We're out in the middle of nowhere, and these orchards go for miles. You drop that bike or crash it, we're hoofin' it out of here. And I gotta say, I ain't feelin' particularly enthusiastic about that option, considerin' Daddy's gonna be out lookin' to tan our hides somethin' fierce."

I slid forward on the motorbike and toed the kickstand

to the up position. I would kill her father before I ever let him lay a hand on her. "How do you start the engine?"

Reaching over, she fingered a metal part on the tank between my thighs. "This is the key. It's turned on already, but you'd turn it if it wasn't. Then you hit the run switch," she patiently explained as she pressed a switch on the right handlebar. "Then the on switch." She pressed another switch.

The engine came to life, and I immediately felt the machine's powerful vibration under me. My life blood pumped through my veins and hummed with anticipation.

She patted my left leg, then squatted. "It's in neutral right now, which means it's not in gear." Taking my boot, she put the toe part over the bar. "In order to make the bike run, you've got to pull the clutch and put it in gear, but not yet, okay?"

I nodded at her instruction.

"Good," she praised absently as she pressed my boot down on the lever. "Feel that click? Now you're in first." She stood. "What you're gonna do now is let the clutch out. Do it nice and slow and simultaneously give the bike gas. Once you start moving, lift your right foot off the ground." She stepped back. "Okay, you got this, baby. You can do it," she praised. "But sweet Jesus, don't drop our bike!"

I did exactly as she said.

As I gave it gas, the bike moved forward, and I lifted my foot.

The heavy machine wobbled and I panicked. Putting my foot back down, I pulled the brake in all at once with my right hand.

The bike jerked to a stop and sputtered right before the engine died.

I frowned.

"No, no, you're doin' good. You just stalled out is all." Coming up beside me, she patted my shoulder. "Everybody does that at first. You got nervous when the gas took, huh?"

I did not answer. I did not have to. She kept talking.

"It's okay. But next time, don't fight with a Harley. It wants to go as much as you want to ride it. Fight the instinct that feels like you'll fall and just give this beast more gas. The faster you go, the easier it is to keep the motorcycle up. Trust me."

Hating that I needed instruction, but appreciating her patience, I tried again.

Going through the steps she'd shown me, I started the bike and put it in gear.

Then I gave it gas.

Except this time, I did not slow start.

I pulled the throttle back harder.

The machine wobbled once, then just as she'd promised, I was moving.

Not moving. Driving.

A motorbike.

Freedom filling my lungs, life blood humming like when I took a woman, anticipation surged to a new level.

I wanted more.

The engine whined, I pulled the clutch and lifted the gearshift. Giving the motorbike more gas, I went even faster.

Then I understood.

This was not simply a motorbike, it was a Harley, and my life until this moment had been a fallacy.

Chapter SEVEN

Shaila

HOLY SHIT, HE WAS DOING IT. He was riding the Hog. And not just riding it, he was driving the hell out of it. His back straight, his shoulders proud, shifting seamlessly, he drove that beauty like he'd been born for it.

Forgetting where we were and what was going on, I whooped with excitement. "Go, baby!"

Driving down the dirt road like he was made for that Harley, my man glanced over his shoulder.

And damn if he didn't smile.

Well, almost. More like the corner of his mouth tipped up, but I was calling it, because holy hell, was he sexy.

I pumped my fist then made a turn-around motion. Cupping my hands, I hollered after him, even though I knew he wouldn't hear me over those dang pipes. "Turn around, practice your turns!"

Nodding once, he slowed the bike down and started to turn. Halfway through, I knew he wasn't gonna make it. He slowed too much, but his foot came down and he kept the bike upright before he stalled it out.

I jogged down to meet him. "Don't worry, turns are hard at first, and this is a narrow lane to try your first turn around in. But you'll get it."

All of a sudden, he went stock-still and looked behind me.

A split second later, I heard it.

Motorcycles. Coming toward us.

"Oh shit." I glanced on either side of us. Orange groves. Dead tree branches. Overgrown grass. I looked ahead. One road.

There wasn't a choice.

"We have to hide." I grabbed one side of the handlebars. "Come on, come on, get off. We'll push it so they don't hear us."

With natural grace, he swung his leg over. "I will push."

I looked behind us as the sound grew closer. "Hurry, they're comin' fast. I'll grab some dead branches."

Tarquin pushed the bike off the road and through the tall grass.

I grabbed a couple dead branches from the opposite side of the lane, then I used them to cover our tracks in the dirt. Hurrying behind Tarquin, there was nothing I could do about the narrow trail of grass the weight of the bike crushed with its tires. Hopefully whoever was coming would be going fast enough not to notice.

Tarq pushed the bike behind an orange tree.

"Lay her down." Upright, she was visible from the road.

Without comment, using his leg to support the bike so it

didn't drop outright, he laid the Hog down on her side. Then he grabbed a gun out of the saddle bag.

I threw the branches over the bike and tried to fluff the grass in the path the bike had made.

"Come," Tarquin calmly commanded as he took my hand and glanced down the road. "Behind this tree." Stepping more over than through the grass, he led us to the next tree further back from the road. "Lie down flat with the earth, perpendicular to the trunk."

I did as he said as the motorcycles engines got louder, but he didn't get down with me. "Where are you goin'?"

Holding out the gun in his hand to me, stock first, he reached for the gun in his back waistband. "Closer to the road."

I took the gun and checked the clip.

"Do not shoot unless we are fired upon first," he commanded. "I do not want to give away our position if we do not have to."

"Don't worry, I'm not startin' anythin' I don't have to." I wasn't looking to add more dark marks against my soul than I had to. When it came time for me to meet my maker, I wanted as few deaths as possible on my hands.

Nodding, he moved toward the tree closer to the road and crouched. Sighting his gun, then looking down the road, he glanced back at me. His eyes so blue in the daylight they were almost clear, he gave me the serious look I was beginning to understand had many shades.

This shade was concern laced with command.

Tipping his chin at the tree as if to say stay down behind it, he turned back to the road as he sank lower into the grass.

On my stomach, holding my arms out in front of me and aiming, I watched dust kick up as two bikers came flying down the old dirt road.

My heart hammering, my nerves pumped, I was primed and ready like a dang charge waiting to blow, but the bikers just rode right past us.

Focused on their unfamiliar cuts that looked like the one Rush had been wearing, I didn't hear Tarquin come up on me.

His hand landed on the small of my back, and I jumped.

"Shh." His heat, his musk, it hit me a second before his breath touched the back of my shoulder. "Do not move."

"I wasn't about to go runnin' out in the road and announce my—"

His hand landed over my mouth. "Stop talking. There is wildlife above you."

My head jerked up.

Then I dropped my gun, and my fingers dug into his arm. *Jesus, Mary and Joseph.*

Three owls. The biggest looking down at us.

His lips touched my ear. "Do not scare them. They are nocturnal. If they take flight, they will give our location away."

I wasn't scared of a whole lot in life.

In fact, before today when I saw twelve bikers facing down my man and my mama, I wasn't scared of nothing except being indentured to a damn biker for the rest of my God-given life. Call me fear averse, or fear-immune, or however you say it, but there was one thing I didn't do.

I did *not* do owls.

No dang way.

Anything that could spin its head around like Satan

wasn't on my short list. It wasn't even in my vocabulary. Add in beaks that could rip your flesh off, and I was out.

My fingers digging deeper into Tarquin's arm, I whispered, "What's your middle name?"

"Middle name?"

"Yeah." I stared at the devil himself disguised as beady yellow eyes and unnatural stillness. "You know, the name between your first and last name."

"I do not have one."

I didn't dare take my eyes off Satan above us to look at him. "Then pick one."

"I do not know any names, and I do not need any other designation."

Jesus fricking Christ. "Then I'll pick one for you."

He said nothing.

Staring at the biggest owl, sure he wanted to eat me, I grabbed the first sentiment that popped into my head. "Eagle." An eagle could kill an owl, or at least chase it away. And sweet mother of Jesus, I wanted a damn eagle to come swooping down right now and use its claws to snatch these creepy-looking suckers up and take them away. Who the hell had yellow eyes anyway?

"I am not an animal of flight."

"Well, you didn't pick a better name. In fact, you didn't pick a name at all, and I needed you to have one for what I'm about to say to you next so you understand the seriousness of the situation."

He said nothing.

I risked taking my eyes off Satan above and grabbed the front of my man's shirt. "Tarquin Eagle Scott, I do *not* do owls."

Chapter

EIGHT

Tarquin

PANIC SAT BETWEEN HER WORDS AS I STARED AT THE COLOR OF her eyes. Spring green edged in the color of earth. My heart pumped faster.

Killing, driving for the first time, bikers after us—unspent adrenaline sat in my veins, and my cock grew hard. "The owl will not harm you."

"*Owls*," she whispered furiously. "As in plural. More than one. And I don't do owls, Tar—"

I did not give her the opportunity to finish her sentence.

I covered her mouth with mine.

She groaned, with protest or approval, I did not know which, but I did not relent.

Driving into her mouth with the hunger of sinful gluttony spoken about in scripture, I did not let up, and I did not retreat as I heard the motorcycle engines change direction.

I claimed her mouth, shoved her shirt up, and unfastened my pants.

Squeezing her breast with one hand, I undid her jeans

with the other. With her hips rising in desperation, I yanked the stiff material I hated down her legs as she kicked off her boots.

The scent of grass, dirt, and orange blossoms mixed with her desire, and I did not check to see if she was wet.

Fisting my cock, I shoved into her tight cunt.

Her back arched, and she moaned into my mouth.

I drove deep with the knowledge that no other woman would ever compare—not that I needed any to. This woman was mine.

Pulling back, I pushed up and braced myself on one hand. Only the head of my cock inside her, her legs spread wide, grass surrounding her, I breathed in and spoke truth. "My body inside you, the earth at your back, no bird will harm you." I would not let it.

"Like an eagle," she whispered. "You've swooped down and taken me."

"I do not have wings." The sound of two motorcycle engines grew closer. "I cannot fly." I shoved deep, dropped my weight onto hers and grabbed my gun. "Do not speak," I warned as I aimed and pulsed inside her.

"*Tarquin.*" She clutched two handfuls of my shirt in panic.

My cock deep inside her, I covered her mouth with one hand and took aim with the other.

The bikers slowed to a stop not five paces from us.

One pointed at the ground. "I'm telling you," he spoke over the sound of the engines. "The tire tracks stop here." He looked in our direction.

My woman stiffened under me.

The second biker pulled out a cigarette and lit it.

I thrust inside her in warning and pressed down harder with my hand over her mouth.

Her core tightened around me.

The second biker inhaled on his cigarette. "And I'm telling you, there's no one out on this road. Prez was crazy sending us out here. You heard Hawkins's old lady. They took off to Kentucky." Taking another drag, he blew out rings of smoke. "They went north, probably on the highway. They got Rush's bike. Who knows how far they could be by now?"

The first man put his kickstand down, turned off his engine, and swung his leg over the motorcycle. Squatting, he looked first up then down the road. "They were here." He stood and kicked at the dirt. "Those are fresh tracks."

Her fingers dug into my chest.

The second man laughed. "You can't tell that."

I held my gun steady.

Her cunt pulsed.

"Can and did." The first biker looked across the road from where we were. "They heard us coming and got out of sight." He drew a gun from his back waistband and glanced at the first biker. "You want to find the prick who killed Rush, or do you wanna sit your fat ass on your Hog and smoke?"

"Fuck you," the second biker clipped as he threw his kickstand down and cut his engine. "I'm only humoring your crazy ass."

"Yeah?" the first biker clipped as he scanned the grove where we were hiding. "Well, humor me further and get your gun ready. I don't feel like getting fucking shot today."

At the biker's last words, my woman flinched under me,

her cunt squeezed my cock, and a twig snapped from the slight shift of her body.

An owl took flight.

"*Motherfucker.*" The first biker fired a wild shot above our heads.

The second biker howled in laughter. "It's a fucking owl, you dick."

Eyes crazed, the first biker swung his aim lower. "Yeah, and what the hell do you think spooked a nocturnal bird, you dumb fuck?"

My woman started to shake.

I sighted my aim.

Her bare thighs tightened around my hips.

"Jesus Christ, relax." The second biker took a drag on his cigarette. "There's no one out—"

"There!" The first biker rushed toward us.

Exhaling, I pulled the trigger.

"Oh fuck!" Too late, the second biker reached for his gun.

The first biker's body hit the ground, another owl took flight, and my woman screamed.

I was already firing my next shot.

The second biker crumpled to the dirt with a bullet hole between his eyes.

I dropped my gun and thrust deep into my woman.

Her fists hit my chest and tears crested her eyes. "I told you, *I hate owls.*"

Pulling back, I drove in hard. "I told you no bird will harm you." My fingers, smelling of gunpowder, found her clit. "Do not scream next time."

Tears fell down her cheeks, her back arched, and she moaned. "It was the owl."

"It was fear." Driving into her tight, wet cunt, I pressed my thumb to her clit. "Come, and do not doubt me again."

Her legs hitched up, and she groaned. "Don't tell me what to do. And I'm not gonna come just because you say—"

I slammed my mouth over hers and I fucked her.

Hard and fast, my body driving into hers, I felt the moment she succumbed to her release.

A tremor went up her back, she cried into my mouth and her cunt constricted all around me.

I released deep inside her.

Chapter Nine

Shaila

Stretching me, smelling like guns and motor oil and grass and dirt, he pounded into me with his giant cock. I never had a chance.

I fell apart.

His back went stiff, and he let go. Pulse after pulse of his hot seed filled my needy pussy, and I shook with an orgasm as my head scrambled.

He'd killed for me.

Again.

With his cock inside me, he'd shot and killed two bikers.

Single-handed.

Bikers wearing cuts from Rush's club.

I hated owls, but I'd lied earlier.

I did have fears.

I feared how much deeper into this whole mess we were getting. I feared my growing feelings for Tarquin. I feared for a future I desperately wanted every time he came inside me. And I feared how long we would be hunted, because I didn't know a single way to get out of having not only Daddy on our tail but another MC wanting us dead.

"Tarquin," I whispered as tears fell down my face. But then I didn't say anything more. I didn't have smart words to sling at him or sass to push against his alphaness. All I had was a quivering pussy that wanted more of his brand of claiming and fear deep in my gut that was making it hard to breathe.

"Do not cry," he quietly commanded as he eased out of me and pushed up to his knees.

His seed rushed out of my body and pooled in the grass below me. "I'm not cryin'," I sniveled. "And you're comin' out of me." I didn't want him to leak out of me. I wanted my body to hold on to every single, precious thing he was giving me. "I don't want you comin' out of me."

With his cock thick and heavy and resting against his still undone jeans, his rough hand grasped my chin, and he tilted my head up. His blue eyes, now more icy than heated, raked over my face. Then he spoke like he knew my very soul. "I will be in you again."

I couldn't stop the sob of fear. "Promise?"

His penetrating gaze didn't waver. "I am not leaving you."

Oh God. He got me. He got me more than any living being had ever gotten me, and I didn't know how it'd happened, but I now needed Tarquin like I needed air to breathe. "Please don't ever break that promise to me."

"I will not." He studied my face a moment then nodded once as if making a decision. "We have to go. The sound of the gunfire will have traveled." Using his strong thighs, he pushed to his full height and tucked himself back into his pants before holding his hand out to me.

I tried to regain some of my composure as I took his hand, but my voice shook. "Why, Mr. Scott, are you being a gentleman now?"

He pulled me to my feet with strength and grace. "I am no gentleman, but I will protect you." He stared into my eyes, and it felt like something shifted between us. "I will always protect you."

I wrapped my arms around him.

I knew we didn't have time. I knew we were now running for our lives. This wasn't just Lone Coaster club business on Daddy's property anymore, where the bodies could be buried and no one would be the wiser. This day had gone from bad to worse, and the second these bodies were found, both of us could spend the rest of our lives in jail.

But in that moment, I needed to feel his arms around me.

Just like I'd needed to feel him come inside me.

I'd needed to feel alive.

Because I hadn't been living.

Not until a six-foot-four blond man with stab wounds and a dislocated shoulder had fallen into my life.

Chapter
TEN

Tarquin

Her arms went around my neck, and her body pressed into mine.

Seeking comfort, she held me tight.

I had never been held tight.

I had never been held.

Before her, no female had sought me out nor given me comfort.

Maybe it was why I had given the female on compound a flower.

Her name, Decima, came to my thoughts, and it felt like a betrayal to the woman in my arms.

I had never wanted Decima. I had never harbored any thoughts of claiming her. I had merely seen her face that day and acted on impulse.

Neither Decima's memory nor her presence when I had been on compound conjured any thoughts close to the ones of fierce protection I was harboring for the woman in my arms.

Holding my woman close for a moment, I allowed the embrace.

Then I took her arms and pulled her off. "We must go." I picked our guns up.

She swiped at her face and spoke with honesty so raw it was sometimes painful to hear. "I think that's the first time you've ever hugged me." She looked up into my eyes, and her voice dropped to a vulnerable whisper. "It felt good."

I took note of her words, her expression and her body language. "It is time to leave. Put your clothes on. I will take care of the bodies."

Nodding, she held her hand out. "Okay, but give me your gun."

I handed it to her.

She used her shirt to wipe the gun down.

I tucked the other gun in my back waistband. "What are you doing?"

"Getting rid of your fingerprints. Cops can track that sort of thing." Still using her shirt, she did not touch the gun with her own hands as she rubbed it once more and set it down in the tall grass. "Besides, this was Rush's gun. We'll leave it here, and with any luck, when they find the bodies, they'll think he was behind this." Picking up her jeans and boots, she dressed. "And since we don't have time to bury them, not to mention we got no shovel, this is the best we can do."

"I will drag the bodies out of sight." Stepping so as not to leave too much of a trail through the tall grass, I walked to the closest biker and grabbed his feet. His weight eclipsed mine, and I could feel the strain in the shoulder my woman had reset for me, but my stab wounds, my bruised ribs and body, those wounds now seemed like a lifetime ago.

Dragging the body a few paces off the road, I let go of him. Returning for the second biker, my woman joined me.

"I'll help." She reached for his wrists.

I was not completely ignorant to the laws outside the fenced perimeter of the compound. Same as on compound, murder was punishable by death. A man had a right to defend himself, this I knew, but proof would lie in the hands of the survivor, and I did not think for one single heartbeat the laws would favor me in this situation.

I did not regret pulling the trigger. I had never regretted pulling the trigger. But seeing my woman struggle to pick up the stone weight of a dead man that I had killed gave me pause.

"Step back," I ordered. "Do not get the blood of my kills on you. Stay pure of this."

Ignoring me, she nodded at his feet. "Grab his ankles and quit puffing your chest out. This ain't nearly the first time I've had blood on my hands, and it sure won't be the last. Besides, you didn't have no reason to kill until you got tangled up with me. So might as well quit your bellyaching over that too, because I ain't got no virtue left."

My jaw ticked, but I picked up his ankles.

We carried the second body and dropped him next to the first.

My woman brushed her hands together then held them up to me. "See? No blood."

I glanced at her, but I did not comment. I was looking at the motorcycles.

"You thinkin' what I'm thinkin'?" she asked.

Not knowing her thoughts, I said nothing.

"I'm thinkin' we got a bike for each of us now." She looked up at me. "You ready for this?"

I did not know how to turn. I did not know how to come to a complete stop without stalling out the engine, and I did not know if my shortcomings would endanger our advance to the cabin. But I did know one thing without doubt. Riding was faster than walking.

I nodded once. "I am ready."

"You gonna be insulted if I suggest you take the smaller bike?"

One bike was white, one was black, but one did not look smaller than the other to my untrained eye. "No."

"Okay, good." She nodded toward the black motorcycle. "Because that Low Rider will be easier on you for turns than the Road King." She grabbed her shotgun and shells out of the side bag on the previous motorcycle and walked toward the white motorcycle. "I'll lead. You stay close, and don't forget to pull the clutch in and put the gear in neutral if you're comin' to a complete stop. Then you won't stall out. Okay?" She shoved the shotgun and ammo in the side bag on the white motorcycle.

I grabbed the backpacks from the old motorcycle and gave her the truth. "I promise nothing until I get more accustomed to the machine." I put the backpacks into the saddle bags on the black motorcycle.

"Harley, baby, say Harley. Or Hog." She swung her leg over the motorcycle. "You remember how to start the bike?"

"Yes." I straddled the one she'd called a Low Rider. "I remember."

Chapter
ELEVEN

Shaila

SEXY AND CONFIDENT, HE STRADDLED THE LOW RIDER AND fired it up.

I started the Road King. It was too much bike for me, but I'd figure it out. We needed to get the hell out of Dodge.

I glanced at him. "Walk the bike through the turn if you need to."

Dominant and all man, he nodded once with the serious intent that made him who he was and revved the engine.

Still feeling him between my legs, gooseflesh skated across my skin. Lord Jesus, help me. Tarquin Scott made me want to make a dozen babies with him. And that wasn't something I needed to be thinking about right now. Getting us to the cabin was priority number one.

Toeing the kickstand, I put the Road King in gear and gave it gas. Swinging a wide arc, I briefly glanced behind me to make sure my man was coming.

Holding the Softail between his legs, he walked it

through a turn around. Then, like he'd been riding for years, he kicked it into gear and hit the gas.

Despite everything, a smile spread across my face. The sun starting to set, a Harley humming under me, an open road—I suddenly wondered why I'd stayed at Mama's as long as I did.

I'd been trapped there as sure as she was trapped in her diseased mind.

Money aside, I could've left. I could've been free....

And I could've never met the man behind me on a Softail.

I glanced behind me again.

Keeping pace, he tipped his chin.

Lord have mercy, the boy was gorgeous. But he wasn't a boy. Tarquin Scott was all man, and God willing he was going to be all mine for a very long time.

Focusing on the road in front of me, I used the rearview mirrors to keep an eye on Tarquin, but I was also looking for more company. As soon as Rush's club brothers figured out the two bikers were missing, they'd come looking. And shoot, I'd forgotten to take their cell phones.

Slowing down, I pulled to a stop.

Wobbling somewhat as he slowed, but not stalling the Softail out, Tarquin pulled up beside me. "What is wrong?"

"We need to go back. I forgot their cell phones. If they're turned on, someone will be able to track them that way."

"We are not going back." Tarquin glanced behind us before looking at me. "The bodies are not buried. They will be easy to find regardless. Flies will have already found them. Turkey vultures are next. They will scent them before sunset.

Wildlife will give away the bodies' location as much as any device to track them."

I stared at him a moment. "How do you know all this?"

He paused. Then he did something he never did when he was speaking to me. He looked away. "I know dead bodies."

Unease crawled up my spine. He wasn't talking about what happened back at Daddy's place. "You care to explain that?"

"We must go. I will explain later."

"Uh-uh." No way. "Explain now." If he was some kind of serial killer or had some sick fetish for dead bodies, I needed to know. I wasn't so far gone that I had to hang on to him. I didn't give the exact location of the cabin. I had my own getaway Harley. If I had to, I could ditch him. I knew I was being somewhat hypocritical after the day's events, but there was killing to protect your own life and there was killing for sport, and there was a huge difference between them.

His clear blue eyes met mine. "I was the digger at River Ranch."

My mind stretched. It knew the word, but for some reason, my brain was misfiring and I wasn't making the connection. "Digger of what?"

"Graves."

And there it was.

His flaw.

The chink in his armor.

The truth of his upbringing.

I knew he wasn't normal. Heck, there wasn't even a normal in my life. And if you looked at this whole thing from a practical perspective, society needed gravediggers. Fact of life, people died, and you couldn't leave bodies lying around just anywhere. You had to bury them.

But Tarquin Scott wasn't no normal gravedigger.

He was a River Ranch gravedigger.

I was sure that didn't involve the sanitized version of regular folk's burials with closed caskets and preserved bodies. And God help me, I was starting to imagine all sorts of places his hands had been before they'd been on my body, and I couldn't go there. That wasn't normal. Thinking that wasn't normal, him being a gravedigger wasn't normal, and not a single damn thing about River Ranch was normal.

"I know what you are thinking," he stated without emotion.

His intense gaze unwavering, his muscles strong, so very strong, probably from digging and lifting dead bodies, and *oh God*. Lord have mercy, he didn't know what I was thinking. No, he surely didn't.

"I bury bodies," he continued. "I do not have a fixation with death."

Okay, maybe he knew what I was thinking.

"Your expression right now is nothing new to me."

Oh sweet Jesus. "Tarquin—"

"River Ranch was not a close community, not like what is spoken of in scripture. It is a closed community. Everything was controlled by oppression, fear, and manipulation. I realized that when I was five turns around the sun. I realize it more now. Socializing was not encouraged but not nonexistent. That said, no one befriended the digger."

My hand went to my chest. "I'm sorry." And I was—for

him, for my thoughts, for the whole situation we were in now.

Stoic, his expression didn't change. "I do not seek nor want your sympathy."

I nodded once. "I understand."

"You cannot possibly understand, not unless you lived it, because not one single thing outside compound gates is the same as inside them. People speak differently, eat differently, behave differently. The landscape is different. The structures are different. Even the air is different. It does not smell of lingering rot, molding wood and decrepit septic systems. Your air is scented with freedom so vast, it is difficult for me to comprehend. Compound life was structured and small. Your life is vast and wild. I had a purpose on compound because everyone was assigned a duty. I did not get to pick. I did not get to protest. And I did not have the luxury of being sensitive to the subject matter. I had a job to do, and I did it. The alternative was to dig my own grave."

I felt ashamed for my earlier thoughts.

"Do not pity me," he clipped, reading my expression as easily as if I had spoken it. "I said I will not leave you, but the moment you pity me is the moment I turn my back on you."

Offended, upset, my mouth opened. "I wasn't sayin'—"

"No, you were not speaking. You were first thinking thoughts of regret for giving yourself to me, then you were pitying my upbringing as if it were not the past."

"I'm so sorry," I whispered.

His jaw ticked, and his knuckles turned white. "Do not be sorry. This conversation needed to occur, and I prefer it to be now than later. We have had it, and if you wish to be my wife, we can move on from it. Decide."

"I... okay." Wow. I took a deep breath. "That's a lot to digest."

"Every word you speak to me is a lot to digest."

Double wow. And I was a terrible person. "Fair enough. I'm sorry."

His jaw tight, his muscles tensed, he held the Softail's handlebars in a punishing grip. "Make a decision. The vultures are here."

I looked up at the quickly fading daylight as the sky turned to dusk. Three large, black birds, majestic but unsteady, teetered across the flaming sunset as their wingspan left brief black smudges in the otherwise picture-perfect sky.

My thoughts jumbled, and my head spun.

But then I did what I always did when I needed to process.

I thought out loud.

Chapter

TWELVE

Tarquin

I SAW IT THE MOMENT I TOLD HER I WAS A DIGGER.
 Regret.
 Her expression took on the mask of wariness I was accustomed to on compound. I was avoided by the brothers, and I was not looked at by the females. Except in the men's quarters after nightly prayer, I was ignored. Then I was the brother who had a reputation for being skilled at mating.
 I had no such reputation now.
 I had nothing now except the woman next to me who rode a motorcycle with more skill than any brother on compound would be able to do. A woman who used words no female would dare whisper on River Ranch.
 But I did not have her if she was going to regret my past and where I came from.
 "Make a decision," I demanded. "The vultures are here."
 She glanced up at the sky. Then she looked back at me. With the hues from the setting sun coloring her face, she began to speak.

Hard JUSTICE

"I didn't have a normal upbringin' either. I don't even know what normal is, and I'm not sure anyone gets that kinda life outside fairy tales and kiddie books meant to make you feel good about the world we live in. So I got no right to hold it against you where you come from or what you went through comin' up. But I can't sit here and look you in the eye and deny I don't worry about what that kinda background means for you and me."

She paused.

I said nothing.

I would not sway her decision. Neither would I give her words of reassurance. I was not River Ranch anymore. I did not have to prove my self-worth to her. She had witnessed my actions today. She knew what I was capable of.

She nodded as if I had spoken. "And I get that me even sayin' those words is hypocritical. I wasn't exactly raised right neither. Seeing my mama OD, knowin' my daddy uses his land as his own personal dumpin' ground for club members he's had enough of, I'm not ignorant. There ain't an untainted single year between us." She glanced at the darkening sky as if seeing the past.

Then she looked back at me. "So I guess it all boils down to one question I got for you."

My muscles coiled, my jaw tight, I tipped my chin.

Her gaze held mine. "Do you believe in love?"

I knew the color of what she was asking. I knew the question she wanted answered without using the direct words to ask if I loved her, but I could not give her the answer she wanted. I could only give her honesty. "I do not know what I believe in." I only knew what I did not believe in—the God she often spoke to, the man who created a compound in the middle of the Everglades, the mercy of humankind. I had no faith in any of those things.

She nodded slowly. Then the female who had given me her virginity, not the woman with a motorcycle between her legs, surfaced. Quiet, hesitant, she asked the question another way. "Do you think you could ever fall in love?"

Seeing her vulnerability made both anger and remorse surface inside me, and I did not have words for the constricting feeling in my chest. I did not like it. Nor did I like the next thought that occurred to me.

It would be easy to tell her what she wanted to hear.

It would be simple to put forth words of untruth and give her affirmation.

It would be effortless to lose all sense of being just and true.

It would be undemanding.

But it would be dishonorable.

I did not tell her what she wanted to hear. "There are no guarantees while we walk this earth. I will not make promises of falsehoods to reassure you. I do not know what the future holds any more than I know the location of your cabin."

She opened her mouth to speak.

I held my hand up. "I am not ignorant. I know what you are asking without using the words directly, but I do not have an answer that will satisfy you. I only have the truth. I have nothing. I have no means. I have no money. I have no shelter with which to house you. I am half a man without those means. But I am no man without my word. I said I would take you as my wife. I gave you that promise with the full knowledge of what that means. I will take care of you. I will tend to you. I will make sure you never go without the necessities of food, water and shelter. But until I get a footing in life outside the perimeter of River Ranch, I cannot guarantee the quality of those necessities."

"I don't need a guarantee on those things. That's not what I'm askin'."

"You are asking if I love you."

Her throat moved with a swallow. "Is that so wrong that I want to know?"

My seed inside her, gunpowder on my hands, I did not know if I resented the question or the circumstances more. "You did not ask this question before."

She glanced behind us as the vultures made their war cry. "Yeah, well, I guess now I asked, but never mind. Forget I said anythin'." She put her motorcycle into gear. "We gotta go."

Without another word, she took off.

I shifted the stolen Harley into first, gave the engine gas and lifted my feet. It was not a smooth start. Unsteady at first, I gave more gas, and just as she had said, the machine was easier to drive at a faster speed.

Quickly shifting into the next gear, giving it more gas, then shifting two more times, I finally matched her speed over the uneven dirt lane.

Wind on my face, the scent of orange blossoms, earth and grass speeding by, I had not known a freedom like this existed. I wanted to keep riding, but we would have to leave the motorcycles once we got deeper into the Glades. As the dirt lane ahead came to a crossroads, I made myself a promise.

One day I would have a machine like this of my own.

Chapter Thirteen

Shaila

We rode for miles until the dirt lane through the groves ended. Despite the heavy bike purring under me, I was still mad as a hornet's nest. I'd given that infuriating man behind me everything I had to give. I had a right to ask any darn question I wanted.

If I wanted to know how he felt about love, then I should be given a straight answer. Not some runaround about no guarantees in life.

I wasn't some sheltered hick. I knew life wasn't fair. More than anyone, I knew that to be true. He didn't have to rub it in my face when I was asking a simple question about how he felt.

Which, fine, he didn't have to answer if he didn't want to.

And I sure as heck wasn't gonna waste any more breath trying to pry it out of him. He could keep his dang feelings if he wanted them so bad. I didn't need them.

Or him.

Anger still simmering, I glanced behind me.

A frown as big as any expression he ever made covered his face as he stared at the approaching crossroads, and I suddenly felt like a jerk for being mad at him. He'd killed for me today. He'd protected me without a single second of hesitation. He wasn't asking nothing of me, and here he was riding a Harley for the first time, worrying about a turn because he ain't never been on a bike.

Sweet Jesus.

Did I really have a right to grill him about something I was pretty damn sure wasn't even in his vocabulary before he got himself beaten and stabbed and thrown out of the only life he ever knew? Of course I didn't.

I came to a stop and cupped my hands at my mouth to holler over the roar of the engines. "Pull your clutch in. Don't stall out!"

Braking much smoother than last time, Tarquin glided the Softail to a stop and came up next to me, putting his feet down.

His voice even, he looked at me without annoyance or anger. "I have not seen anyone behind us yet."

"Me neither." I'd been checking my rearview mirror, worrying who'd be after us by now.

"You were angry with me," he stated without preamble.

Shaking my head, I smiled without humor. "I can't get nothin' past you, can I?"

"No," he replied before giving me another peek into his past. "When no one speaks to you, you learn to read expressions. They are more telling than words."

"Well, I'm sure my expression said I was hopin' you'd

declare your undyin' love for me forever and ever." I let out an awkward half snort, half laugh.

He didn't even smile. "There is nothing I dislike about you."

I felt guilty all over again for being mad at him. Embarrassed, ashamed, I didn't know what I was, but stupid words came out of my mouth. "Be still my heart."

"I am not making a joke."

Inhaling a lungful of fresh air laced with citrus blooms, I told myself to get a grip. "I'm sorry. Just ignore me. It's been… quite a day." I glanced up and down the road. "So we got two choices from here," I began, trying to change the subject and get out of the uncomfortable mess I'd created. "We can—"

"I will never ignore you."

God help me, my heart tripped. Worse, the seriousness of his tone and expression made me feel like it was an opening to get him to share more of his feelings. But I wasn't gonna pry the lid off another can of worms with a game of twenty questions, so I just gave him my gratitude. "Thank you. I appreciate that."

His gaze intent on me, he stared. Then after a beat, he nodded once. "You are welcome. What are our options?"

For a long moment, all I could do was stare back at him.

The perfectly sharp angles to his face, his sun-streaked blond hair, the muscles in his shoulders as he held his bike—he was so intense and so beautiful, I was questioning whether I deserved his attention at all.

Telling myself it was fate that brought us together, I swallowed past a lump in my throat and ignored the heat between my legs that never seemed to go away anymore whenever he was near. "Okay. There's two ways to get to the cabin from here. We can take the road goin' south. It swings behind my daddy's property, and it's the shortest way to get there. Or we can go north, make a big loop through Homestead, then come at the area the cabin is in from the north. It'll be a bit of a longer hike once we're on foot, but we won't be skirtin' Daddy's property."

"The north route," he answered without hesitation.

"Well," I hedged, "here's the issue with the north way. We'll be goin' on county and state roads, and we're drivin' two stolen bikes. If we get pulled over or spotted, we're toast."

Glancing first south, then north, his gaze came back to mine. "How crowded will the roads to the north be?"

"This time of day?" I shrugged. "No tellin'. Not many people live out here, but it's quittin' time, and people'll be comin' and goin' as they leave work and head home."

"What if we wait until well past nightfall?"

I shrugged again. "Less traffic. But that'll also make us more visible. We don't have any helmets, so two blonds on bikes? Rush's club is probably already lookin' for us."

He thought for a moment. "The cabin is in a secure location?"

"I think so. As long as we don't lead anyone toward it. No one I know has any idea about it, as far as I can tell. I think Daddy would've mentioned it before now if he knew it was there. He would've warned me off it or warned the bikers about it when they came for barbeques on the property. He would've told them to stay away from it. I figure if someone knew about the place, I would've heard mention of it, but I never have."

"If we leave the motorcycles where they can be discovered, it will lead them in that general direction."

I smiled. I couldn't help it.

His eyebrows drew together. "What?"

"You said motorcycle instead of motorbike."

His shoulders lifted with an inhale, but he otherwise ignored my grin. "I think we should go north after nightfall and take the time between now and then to dispose of one of the motorcycles where it will not lead to the cabin's location."

"That's a solid plan, but I think I got a better one." I smiled. "Hear me out?"

Chapter
FOURTEEN

Tarquin

SHE SMILED. It was without any pretense or motive. Pure of heart, it was a smile of innocence, and I did not want any other man seeing it.

"Explain," I demanded, the urge to take her again already sharp.

"Okay, well. remember how I told you Rooney at work can get anything, and he got you your antibiotics?"

I already disliked her plan. "We should not reveal our whereabouts to anyone."

"No, no, nothin' like that. We'll go to him."

I shook my head. "No. It is not safe."

She held a hand up. "Just hear me out. Rooney is such an obvious choice, they won't think to look for us there. Mama will have told Daddy that we're headin' to Kentucky, and if we keep to the same plan of goin' north, but stop by Rooney's, we'll just let the same information slip, and it'll only solidify our story. But more, Rooney isn't only good for gettin' things that you can't otherwise normally get. He fences stuff too. Let's give him the Road King and take some cash for it. It's a win-win."

I hated the idea. "No."

"What do you got against money? It's not like we have any." Her eyes narrowed more with challenge than suspicion. "Unless you've been holdin' out on me?"

"The only thing of value I had, I gave to you."

She frowned. "You did?"

"My knife." The knife the same brother who had made me memorize the address had given me. The knife he had put in my hand when I had thought I would draw my last breath.

"Oh!" She pulled it out of her pocket and ran her thumb over the ornate handle before handing it to me. "It's a beautiful knife. Thank you… for trusting me with it."

Holding the motorcycle steady, I nodded and secured the knife in my pocket. "I do not have anything against money. I know it is a necessity, but not at the expense of your safety."

"My safety?" She looked surprised. "What about yours?"

I did not address her question. "We are not doing it."

She sighed. "Okay, look, if we wind up needing to actually run, as in not stay at the cabin, we're gonna need cash. This is the only way I know how to get some other than what I took from work before I hightailed it out of there."

"Then we already have some money."

She smirked. "You can never have too much money."

Thirsty, hungry, on edge, I did not want to argue with her. "I am not discussing it further."

"Okay, great, it's settled. We'll head north, find a place

to pull off the road and get the bikes hidden. When it's well and truly dark, we'll go to Rooney's and get rid of this beast." She patted the bike between her thighs. Then she taunted me. "Unless you're worried about ridin' that Softail on the main roads?"

My jaw ticked. I did not comment.

"Okeydokey then," she said cheerfully. "It's settled. Follow me."

Before I could protest, she was off.

I put my motorcycle into gear and gave it gas.

The initial start smoother than the previous ones, it was almost enough of a rush to have me forget my anger at her plan to put herself in danger.

Following her, I made a wide but relatively smooth turn onto the paved road before shifting through the gears and catching up to her. I still could not reconcile a female on a motorcycle, but with my woman's hair blowing behind her and the confidence in her posture, it was hard to deny she belonged on the Harley.

The wind rushing by, the power of the machine, the speed, it was intoxicating like I would imagine a drug to be.

I did not want to quit this feeling.

I wanted to keep riding.

But I could not forget what had transpired today.

As soon as the last two bodies were discovered, we would be hunted by more than just her father.

We needed to get off this paved road.

Chapter

FIFTEEN

Shaila

I LED US AS FAR NORTH AS I DARED BEFORE TURNING OFF THE county road into an old hunting preserve. Even though I'd lived in this area for years, I rarely left Daddy's property. Daddy used to take me riding when I was younger, and he'd take this very route. Sometimes he'd take me into Miami proper and take me shopping or to a sit-down restaurant to eat.

But the past few years, those trips had become so infrequent that I'd stopped expecting them. And the last time he took me to eat, we didn't even take Daddy's Street Glide. One of the Lone Coasters who'd been driving Daddy around for a year drove us. Using his rearview mirror, the jerk eyed me in the back seat the whole time. Daddy pretended like nothing was wrong, and he never mentioned it, but next time he came to visit me and Mama, he had a new driver. I never saw that jerk who'd eyed me again. Not even at one of the barbeques Daddy hosted out at the house.

Driving around the chained, single-arm gate that blocked

the road into the preserve, I glanced behind me to make sure Tarquin made the turn without incident, but I shouldn't have worried. He'd taken to riding like a fish to water.

I drove around back of the single building that housed a public restroom and cut the engine on the Road King.

Tarquin pulled up beside me and smoothly glided to a stop without stalling out his Softail before cutting his engine.

I smiled at him in the post twilight darkness. "Good job."

He put the kickstand down and swung his leg off the bike like he'd done it a million times. "Good job doing what? I have done nothing."

He'd protected me, learned to ride, made love to me, and saved my life, all in a day's work. I fought a sarcastic smirk and tried instead to learn a taste of his kind of honesty. "Riding. You did good today."

Pausing in his scan of our surroundings, his gaze cut back to me. "What is inside this building?"

For a second, he threw me. The two doors in front with the little pictures of the filled-out stick figures of a man and woman were self-explanatory to me. But that didn't mean it was how they did things at River Ranch. "Restrooms. One marked for boys and one marked for girls. Did you have unisex bathrooms at River Ranch?"

He shook his head once and resumed scanning. "The females had their own facilities in the women's quarters."

"And you?"

"The men had their own in the men's quarters."

"So you like, what, all bunked together?"

He walked to the edge of the building and scanned the

road coming in even though we hadn't passed another soul out here for miles. "Mostly."

I waited, but he didn't elaborate. "So you had roommates? Kinda like the barracks in the military?" I'd read about that in one of my history books.

His gaze cut north. "I am familiar with the term, but I do not know specifically what the military does."

"Soldiers all room together, in training, in battle. Sometimes buildings, sometimes tents."

He turned to face me, and I was taken aback again by how striking he was.

His eyes almost looked clear in the moonlight shining down on his face. "Then, yes, it was like that. Some of the men, the elders and the hunters, had their own quarters. It was a hierarchy system. The higher up your post, the more privilege you received. As a digger, I did not warrant private quarters."

Curiosity got the best of me. "What if you claimed a woman?"

"I would have claimed a female, not a woman," he corrected. "And if I won rights, then I would have been granted private quarters to occupy." He looked to the south.

"Did they have their own bathroom?" I couldn't imagine sharing a bathroom.

"A toilet and a sink. Showers used too much water for the septic system on site, so they were off system behind the quarters."

I frowned. "Off system? So what, you like showered outside?"

He nodded once.

"Every day?" That sounded like camping, and not dissimilar to what we'd have to do at the cabin. Which, now that it was getting close, the very idea of it was starting to sink in, and I didn't think I'd fully prepared myself for the reality of that.

He stopped scanning our surroundings and focused his gaze back on me. "I do not understand the question."

"Every time you wanted to shower, you did it outside? No matter the weather?" He was so close, I could reach out and touch him, but I didn't.

His arms at his side, his body still, he made no move to touch me either. "Yes."

I rubbed my hand over my throat. "We're gonna have to do the same at the cabin," I admitted.

His eyes tracked the movement of my hand. "I did not think any different."

Oh Lord, thinking about the shower made me realize the other issue. The big issue. "So, um, there's no toilet at the cabin." And when it was just me going there, I didn't think it'd be that big a deal. I'd even practiced doing my business in the woods and covering it up afterward. I figured it wouldn't be too bad a tradeoff for freedom until I could figure out a long-term plan, or until Daddy gave up looking for me, thinking I was either dead or gone.

But staring at a man who was well over six feet, it made the situation... bigger.

"When you said the cabin had a well pump outside, I did not presume there would be any indoor plumbing." His voice calm and steady, he gently grasped my wrist and brought my hand off my throat before letting go of my wrist.

The single touch made my nerves sing. "So, we'll have to…" I waved my hand around awkwardly. "You know. Outside." I blushed, hard.

As if seeing my embarrassment, he swept a single finger across my cheek. "I am aware."

Despite my jacket, I shivered. "That doesn't bother you?" I mean, I'd stocked toilet paper. And I'd heard you could use leaves in a pinch, and oh sweet Jesus, I didn't even know how I was having a conversation about this, let alone thinking about it when he was looking at me like he was.

His gaze dropped to my lips. "There are many worse things."

The air between us suddenly too warm, his comment too close to home, I stepped back and tried not to think of his hands on me or what would happen to us if Daddy or Rush's club found us. Needing to change the subject, I blurted out the first thing that came to mind. "Did any of the men try to claim a female just so they could get private quarters?" Saying female and quarters in any other conversation would have seemed out of place, but with Tarquin, the words rolled off my tongue as if I'd been using them to describe women and housing my whole life. Maybe that should've bothered me, but like he'd said, there were many worse things.

Walking behind me, he scanned the other side of the building. "I am sure that was the motivation behind some of the men's attempts."

"Attempts?" I asked, not sure I wanted to hear the answer.

"Not many men survived the claiming rights."

Oh dear Lord. "Meanin'?"

He came back to stand in front of me. Picking up a strand of my hair, he glanced at it as he spoke. "Meaning many died trying."

I swallowed past a sudden lump in my throat. When I spoke, my voice was as unsure as I felt asking a question I didn't really want the answer to. "Then you had to bury them?"

Nodding once like he wasn't affected by the whole thing, he slid his hand down the strand of my hair he had caught between his thumb and first two fingers. "I have never seen hair your color."

"It's natural," I defended, not sure why I was bothering.

"Why would it not be?"

"Some women dye their hair." Sweet Jesus, there was so much he didn't know about the world, that if I stopped to think about it, it'd overwhelm me faster than a semi with no brakes.

"I do not want you to ever dye it."

A half laugh, half unladylike snort came out, because that's what he did to me. This man made me nervous like nobody's business. "I don't plan on it. Except maybe when I'm old and gray, then maybe I'll dye it back to its original color so you don't leave me for some young thing with pretty strawberry-blonde hair."

"Is that what your hair color is called?" He didn't address the leaving me comment.

"Yes." I wanted him to address that comment. I wanted him to deny it because everything about him made me crazy with jealousy.

"Strawberries are bright red."

"Yes, they are. There's no accountin' for the English language, is there?"

He didn't answer. He fingered another strand and stared at me.

When he looked at me like this, like I was the only person in the world, I didn't have words to describe that kind of sense of belonging. He made me feel like I was the most important thing to him with a single look. I wasn't naïve. I knew he could have any woman. And maybe from an outsider's perspective, it'd seem like he needed me more than he wanted me, because of where he'd come from and everything he didn't have.

But in truth, this man standing in front of me was a thousand times tougher than my own daddy, and until I'd dragged him clear across the swamp, I'd never met anyone tougher than my daddy.

And he didn't need me.

As much as that stung when he'd said it, I needed to remember it, because there was no better soothing balm for my unfounded jealousy when it came to him than those very words.

Tarquin Scott did not need me.

He *chose* me.

He chose to be standing right here, right now, and he chose to tell me he'd never seen hair my color before. That was Tarquin-speak for feelings.

And I needed to embrace it.

Yes, there were a million questions I wanted to ask him and a million more answers I wanted to know about him and his life and everything in between, but more than anything, in this moment, I hoped he saw in me what I was seeing in him.

"Thank you," I said quietly, not sure how else to say my heart was full.

"I did not do anything."

"You saved my life today." Those men in the groves would've killed us as sure as daylight.

"You saved mine," he countered.

A shy smile touched my lips. "Now we're even?"

"I will never take count nor tally."

My heart slipped even further away from my grasp. "Is it too early to tell you how I feel?" Would it scare him away? Turn him off? Make him angry?

"You may always tell me how you feel."

Maybe I should've kept my mouth shut. Maybe I should've waited. Maybe I should've done a million things different, but I didn't hesitate with what I did next because I needed to get the words out. I needed them to be free and out in the open, and I needed them to be heard in case I never got another chance to say them.

"I love you, Tarquin Scott."

His hand, rough and warm and sure, cupped my face. Then his voice dropped to the deepest, sexiest kind of rumble I ever did hear, and he laid a truth on me I didn't see coming.

"I have never kissed another woman."

Fire and ice.

Bitter and sweet.

Pain and joy.

Every conflicting emotion hit me all at once, but none more profound than a single word he let slip.

Woman.

Woman.

His last word replayed in my head, eclipsing the heartfelt sentiment he'd given me before that single word destroyed everything, because all I could think of was its meaning to him.

He didn't say female.

He'd said woman.

And he'd said it on purpose because Tarquin Scott never spoke an untrue word.

"I...." My mouth opened, I started to speak, but then I couldn't say anymore because the heart I'd just given away was breaking from a brand of jealously that hurt too bad to think about.

His thumb stroked my cheek. "That upsets you."

Mud on my pretty boots upsets me.

The baby bird who flew into my bedroom window last month upset me.

Mama getting high every night upset me.

Tarquin Scott sleeping with countless women before me didn't upset me, it devastated me.

I wanted him to be mine alone.

I was his alone.

But I couldn't undo the past no more than I could undo who my heart decided to fall in love with.

"Yes," I admitted. "It upset me that you said woman." I dropped my gaze. "I know what that means."

Grasping my chin, he tipped my face up. "It means that I have not ever taken another woman's mouth."

Oh God, that hurt. "But you've taken other women." My traitorous eyes welled, and a tear fell as my voice broke. "Lots of other women." I pulled out of his grasp.

Chapter SIXTEEN

Tarquin

SHE PULLED OUT OF MY GRASP, AND I LET HER.

Betrayal I could not rectify shown on her face. "I am not apologizing for my past."

"I'm not askin' you to." Her back to me, she reached for the side bag on her motorcycle as mosquitoes swarmed overhead.

"We should take shelter inside the building." It would become uncomfortable soon, and there was nothing more I could say out here that would ease her emotions surrounding my past.

"That buildin' is locked." Searching through the side bags, she came away with a metal flask, opened it, sniffed it and made a sound of disgust before emptying the contents in the dirt.

"What are you doing?"

"Keepin' myself from makin' the same bad decisions as my mama. I don't need alcohol, and neither do you."

I had never had alcohol, but I did not argue. It was not allowed on compound and everyone was warned of not only the ill effects of consumption, but the repercussions if caught with it. "Wait here." I walked toward the front of the building.

Two locked doors, a metal sink with a spigot on the wall between them, and higher up where you could not see in were openings for windows that were covered with screens instead of glass.

My woman came up behind me and went to the sink. "Thank God for water fountains." She turned the handle and water bubbled up. Letting it run a moment, she drank from it, then rinsed out the flask and filled it. "Here." She handed it to me.

I took it and drank all the water from it.

Without comment, she refilled it and held it out again for me.

I drank, then handed it back to her. "Thank you."

"More?"

"No, thank you." I glanced from the water fountain to the screened opening, then I pulled out my knife and tested the strength of the fountain with my foot.

"What are you doing?"

"Getting us shelter." Using the fountain for leverage, I grasped the window's ledge and pulled myself up. Two quick slices with my knife, and the screen gave way.

"Sweet Jesus," my woman murmured. "Add breaking and entering to our growin' list."

I crawled through the opening and landed in a darkened room that smelled of septic and disinfectant. By the light of the moon, I found the door and unlocked it. Pushing it open, I gave my woman a command. "Come inside."

"Well, with that kinda invitation, how can a woman

resist?" With a natural sway in her hips that women on compound did not have, she walked inside.

I shut and locked the door. "There will be fewer mosquitos in here. We will be more comfortable."

"I'm not sure I ever equated a public restroom with comfort before, but I can't deny the truth of what you're sayin'." She eyed the toilet.

Reading her body language, I tipped my chin. "Go ahead."

Her eyebrows shot up. "In front of you?" She laughed uncomfortably. "Yeah, no. That ain't happenin'."

If this were a female on compound, I would have commanded her to do as I said, and she would have done it. But this woman was unlike any woman I had ever encountered.

"I will give you privacy," I conceded.

Unlocking the door, I stepped out and went back to the motorcycles. Hungry, I searched all the side bags, but all I came up with were some tools, cigarettes, and what looked like a pair of pants and a jacket to wear in the rain. Slipping one of the guns in my waistband, I heard the toilet flush, and I went back inside.

My woman was standing at the sink rinsing a piece of material I recognized.

I stated the obvious. "If you did not wear undergarments, you would not have to wash them."

She looked over her shoulder at me. "If I didn't wear *undergarments*, I'd be standin' here rinsin' my jeans out, and that'd be a whole heck of a lot more uncomfortable to wear soakin' wet."

I did not respond. I leaned against the wall and watched her.

"Figures you got nothin' to say to that." She returned her attention to her task. "You're not the one rinsin'."

Her hips full, her body curved like no woman I had ever seen, she was every desire I did not know I had wanted before a fortnight ago. Aroused, I stepped behind her and leaned my chest into her back.

She flinched. "Don't sneak up on me in the dark like that."

I covered her hands with mine and took the material from her as my body surrounded hers.

Stiff at first, she yielded to my presence. Then her voice softened. "What are you doin'?"

Her hair brushing against my face, her scent in my head, I rinsed the material and spoke quietly against her ear. "I do not want you wearing undergarments. I do not want you in pants when you are not on a motorcycle. I do not want you to confuse my past with my commitment to you, and I do not ever want your hair tied back."

Chill bumps arose on her neck, and she exhaled slowly through her mouth. Gripping the edge of the sink, she inhaled deeply and exhaled slowly two more times before she spoke. "I don't know what you've done to me, but when you touch me like this, speak to me all quiet-like, I want to do whatever you say only so you'll keep touchin' me. *Sweet Jesus*, I want you to keep touchin' me."

"Did you hear what I said?"

Her body stilled. "I heard."

"Do you understand?"

Her voice quieted. "Yes."

"I will always tend to you." I could not stop myself from touching her now if I wanted to.

"Is that a promise?"

"Yes." I shut off the water and wrung out the material before placing it on the edge of the sink. "Are you sore?" I wanted to come again, but more, I wanted to make her release. I wanted to show her my past was behind me, and that she was my present.

She paused. "I'm good."

"You hesitated." Brushing her hair aside, I touched my lips to the back of her neck.

She shivered. "I'm fine."

"Unbutton your pants and push them down, then grasp the sink again." I kissed the other side of her nape. She smelled most like herself where her hair hid the soft skin of her neck. Warm, female, flowers I had never scented in real life—I dreamt of her scent.

"Here?" she asked anxiously. "You want me to push my pants down in a public restroom?"

"You have already done it."

"Y-Yes, but I was…." She cleared her throat. "That was different."

I wanted to take her hard and rough. I wanted to mark her flesh with my teeth. I wanted to release inside her over and over. But that was not what this was about right now. "Unbutton them. Now."

"Yes, sir." Her words gave me attitude, but her voice shook as she unbuttoned her jeans and pushed them down a mere few inches.

I slid my hands down the length of her arms, then I grasped her waist before slipping my fingers between the material in my way and her soft skin. Her heart beat faster as I pushed her pants over her hips and down her thighs.

I stilled my palm flat on her stomach. "Do you know what I expect?"

"No," she whispered.

"When I am tending to you, I expect you to do what I say, as I say it, without hesitation."

"You may want that, but I—"

I shoved two fingers inside her.

She jerked in my embrace and let out a yelp.

"Without hesitation," I repeated. "Do you understand what that means?" I stroked inside her front wall where I knew she would feel it most.

"I—*ohhh*." She pushed her hips back into mine and ground against my hardness.

I grabbed her waist with my free hand and held her at a distance from me. "Do you understand?"

"Yes, yes, yes," she moaned, rubbing against my hand. "Please don't stop."

"Tell me what it means, woman," I demanded, maintaining pressure inside her.

Her knees bent, and her back arched. "Oh God, it means, it means…" She sucked in a sharp breath as I increased the pressure. "It means I do what you tell me."

"It means you are submissive," I corrected, stroking my thumb across her clit once.

"I don't know what you're doin' to me, but sweet Jesus, please don't stop."

"Are you going to do what I say from now on?"

"Yes, please God, *yes*."

I stroked hard inside her at the same time as I rubbed a circle on her clit. "Come now."

Her hands left the sink and gripped my wrist as she bent at the waist. She let go with a moan that was part desperate cry, part whimper, and constricted around me.

My cock throbbed, and my balls drew tight as her release pulsed around my fingers.

"Tarquin, oh my God, *Tarquin.*"

I stroked her until her cunt stopped pulsating.

Biting her ear, I withdrew my fingers. Then I said something I had never said to another woman. "I want you to swell with my child."

Chapter Seventeen

Tarquin

"Oh, *sweet Jesus*." Shaking, short of breath, she gripped the sink. "You can't say things like that to me after doin' things like that to my body."

I would say what I wanted, when I wanted to her. "You will swell with child." I had already come inside her several times.

"Not if you keep holdin' back from me, I won't." She pulled up her pants and fastened them.

"I was not holding back from you."

She turned to face me. Her face flushed, she looked up at me with more shyness than attitude. "Then what were you doin'?"

"Giving you a release."

Her eyebrows drew together. "Without givin' yourself one?"

My arms at my sides, my cock painfully hard, I let my gaze fall to her erect nipples. "I have not been making myself release." I wanted to take her rough and hard until her cunt constricted around my cock in another orgasm. "You have been doing that."

Her face flushed deeper, and her voice dropped to a whisper. "I like doin' that."

"I know."

For three heartbeats, she stared at me. Then she looked away. "You're not kissin' me or holdin' me."

"I am also not fucking you." I could not erase my past, but I could show her how I would tend to her.

A smile touched her lips. "You don't usually use that word." She blushed. "I like it." Seriousness took over her expression, and she looked back up at me. "But how come you ain't takin' me?"

"I felt how swollen your cunt was earlier. I tasted the cry on your lips when I entered you. Despite you telling me you are fine, I know you are sore. I am giving your body a rest before I release inside you again."

She bit her lip. "How much of a rest?"

"Until tomorrow."

"I may be inexperienced compared to you, but I ain't naïve."

"Meaning?"

She glanced down at my hard length pressing against my jeans. "Meanin' I know there are other ways to get a release. I may have never done anythin' like that, but I can learn."

The thought of her on her knees with her hair in my hand and my cock in her mouth made me harder. And knowing I would be the first man to be in her mouth made me possessive. But I did not reach for her. "Not tonight."

She frowned. "Why?"

"Because I need to stay alert." If I released again, I wouldn't be.

"And not comin' is gonna make you alert?"

"No." The painful erection straining my pants would. "Have a seat and get some rest." It was going to be a long night before we made it to the cabin.

"Sit?" She looked affronted. "On a public restroom floor?"

"Yes."

Her face twisted with disgust. "Do you know what happens on these floors? It already smells like an outhouse in here. I'm not puttin' my backside or anythin' else anywhere near that floor. Nope, I'll stand, thank you very much."

I stared at her a moment, but she simply stared back in defiance.

I picked her up.

"Hey!" she yelped. "What are you doin'?"

One arm under her knees, the other behind her back, I sat down and leaned against the wall. "Close your eyes."

"Is this your way of gettin' me on the floor?"

"Yes."

Keeping her feet tucked together, she leaned into my chest. "Well, it's workin'."

"Good."

She was quiet a moment, and despite the pounding need to release, I closed my eyes.

"You think God knows we killed those men today in self-defense?" she asked after a long moment.

"I do not know what God thinks." Or if there was a God, but I did not say that thought aloud.

"I'm hopin' he does. I mean, it was us or them."

I did not disagree.

She pulled back from my chest and looked up at me. "You're not sayin' nothin'."

"What is there to say? If I did not pull the trigger first today, I would be dead and you would have been sold."

Her voice quieted. "Do you have any regrets?"

"No."

"Do you think we'll still get into heaven?"

I stared at her pretty green eyes for a moment. In the moonlight streaming in through the screened window, they were forest green, not new leaf green, but they were no less pretty. "I think it feels like heaven when I am inside you."

A smile spread across her face. "Why, Tarquin Scott, be still my heart."

"Why do you do that?"

Her smile faded. "Do what?"

"Use both a first and last name at the same time." I was the only other person in the room. I was the only Tarquin I knew. I was the only Tarquin she knew. "What is the purpose of using two names when one suffices?"

She thought a moment, then she shrugged. "I really don't know. For emphasis, I think. Or maybe it's just a Southern thing, being formal and all." She laughed once. "I honestly don't know why I do it. When my mama was mad at me growing up, she'd use my first and middle name together. That's how I knew I was in serious trouble."

"You have a third name?"

"Yep, Shaila Victoria Hawkins."

I said the middle name to myself, rolling around the

unusual combination of letters. "What is the purpose of the third name?"

She shrugged and leaned back into my chest. "To sound pretty, I guess. Tradition too. And sometimes in certain religions, when you decide to take Jesus into your heart, you take on a confirmation name."

I did not understand any of it, nor see the purpose of it. "I am not an eagle."

She giggled as her finger traced a vein on my forearm. "Now that I've had time to think about it, no, you most certainly are not. You're a ground animal. One that runs fast and swift and can snatch its prey before the poor victim even knows what hit him."

Not knowing if I was insulted or flattered, I probed at her assessment. "Is that what you think of me?"

"Oh yes." She nodded with conviction. "Most definitely. You're like a cougar... no, a panther. A Florida panther. Sleek and fast and cunning."

"I am none of those things."

"You are to me," she quietly admitted.

I entertained a thought I had had earlier in the day. "You are neither earth, nor water, nor air." I stroked her blonde hair with red hues. "You are fire."

She leaned away from my chest, and for long moment she simply stared at me, and I held her gaze. Then a shy smile softened her face. "I think I like you, Mr. Scott."

"You more than think," I corrected.

Her smile widened. "Do me a favor?"

Making no such commitment, I tipped my chin for her to continue.

"Don't ever change." She kissed my cheek. "Stay true, Tarquin Scott."

Unable to make any such assurances, I gave her the one thing I could promise her. "I will always give you my honor and my strength."

"*Honor and strength*," she whispered, repeating my words.

"Yes."

"And your love?" she asked hopefully. "Will you give me that?"

I wrapped my arms around her tight, but I did not hide the slight twitch at the corner of my mouth. "Close your eyes, woman. It is going to be a long night."

A smile in her voice, she gave me the same attitude that had made me think of her as not earth, water or air, but fire. "*Yes, sir.*"

Chapter

EIGHTEEN

Shaila

I peeked in the grungy window of Rooney's trailer. TV blasting, a blunt between his lips, he was sitting on a couch you couldn't pay me to touch.

I glanced over my shoulder at Tarquin, who was standing behind me with a gun in his hand and a scowl on his face as he scanned the trailer park. Or rather, the vacant lot where a few rusted-out trailers were squatting next to piles of trash that made the county dump look like a picnic.

"We're good," I whispered. "He's alone."

Tarquin glanced at the Road King we'd glided in and hidden behind Rooney's trailer. "I do not like this plan."

I patted him on the chest. "Too late. We're here and startin' up the bike now to drive away will only get us more attention than we want. Besides, you got a gun and you know how to use it." I smiled. "Trust me, you already have the upper hand on Rooney." I headed toward the front of the trailer.

Tarquin caught my wrist. "What if he alerts someone?"

Awareness shot up my arm. Every time he touched me,

my body came alive and all I could think about was how it felt when he was tending to me.

Tending.

Mentally shaking my head, I still couldn't believe I was speaking like him now.

Forcing myself to focus, I got back on track. "Who's Rooney gonna call? His best friends are junkies and drug dealers, and none of them are gonna bother with the likes of us." I hoped.

Tarquin glanced at the other trailers before his gaze cut back to me. "Remember the plan."

"I remember, but I don't like it." If anything went south, I was to get out and leave him behind to handle everything on his own. "If we're supposed to be partners, we're supposed to help each other."

A scowl overtook his face, and sweet Jesus, it made him even more handsome. Threatening, but handsome. "We are not partners. You are my woman. I will protect you. End of discussion."

"Lord have mercy," I muttered. "It's a good thing I grew up around bossy men like you, you know that?" I didn't wait for a response. "Otherwise, I might actually take offense at that kinda talk. Now come on, we got some money to make."

His jaw ticked, like it did when he wasn't happy, but he followed me to the front door.

Not bothering to knock, because I knew Rooney kept his place unlocked, I took the two rickety steps and pushed his door open.

Before I could say a word, Rooney held his hand up. "Wait, this is the best part." His back to us, he stared at the

TV as some big explosion on screen happened. "That's what I'm talking about!" Rooney whooped.

Tarquin stepped in behind me and quietly closed the door. Ever alert, he was already scanning the small, smelly place like he'd scanned the outside.

"Rooney," I clipped, already out of patience.

"Yeah, yeah, coming." Setting his blunt in an overflowing ashtray, he reached for a remote and turned the TV down. "What can I get for—" His eyes landed on me, and he stopped midsentence as his jaw dropped.

Then he turned dead white.

"No. *No way in hell.* You can't be here, Shaila." Looking way less stoned than when we walked in, Rooney's head started to shake like a bobble toy. "You need to leave. Like *right* now. Your dad's gonna kill me. And I do mean kill, with a capital *K*." His nervous gaze cut to Tarquin, then his eyes went even wider. "And holy fuck, Shaila! *Is that him?*" His voice squeaking on his last words, he sounded like he was being strangled.

"Him who?" I asked with a smirk. "If you mean, is that my husband, then yep, sure is. And we're goin' to Kentucky, and we need—"

"LA LA LA LA!" Rooney yelled, slamming his hands over his ears. "For Christ's sake don't tell me where you're going! Stone will beat it out of me!" Spinning in a circle, he bent at the waist. *"He'll kill me."*

"Shaila," Tarq quietly warned.

I held a hand up to him. "I got this." I pulled Rooney's hand off his ear. "You wanna make some money or what?"

Half bent, holding his stomach like he was gonna be

sick, Rooney turned his head to look up at me. "You're crazy. Leave."

"A lot of money," I corrected. "More than you'll ever make selling to strung-out junkies who pay you in roadkill and stolen oranges."

Rooney shot upright and held a finger up. "One time, Shaila, *one time* I took that deer. Meat is meat. You know how long that fed me for? Don't act like you didn't eat some too."

Tarquin interrupted Rooney's rant. "We are out of time."

"Do you want a brand-new Road King or what?" I asked Rooney.

He blinked. Then he blinked again. "Say what?"

"A Harley." I threw my hands up. "Don't you know what a Road King is? You been livin' under a rock?" As soon as the words left my mouth, I felt like a heel. Looking over my shoulder at Tarq, I apologized. "Sorry. No offense meant."

Giving me a tight nod, he didn't say nothing.

I looked back at Rooney. "A brand-spankin'-new Road King with all the bells and whistles. Retails for thirty-five grand easy." Maybe, probably. Close enough. "All we want for it is however much cash you got on you."

"And food," Tarquin added.

"And food," I agreed. "But nothin' homemade from this pigsty. Real food in unopened packages. So how much cash you got?"

Rooney stared at me like I'd lost my ever-loving mind. "Are you insane?"

"Possibly." At the mention of food and the thought of potato chips, I was suddenly starving. "So what's it gonna be?

Because if you ain't interested, I got another buyer waitin' to take this beast off my hands, but since we worked together, I came here first out of courtesy. I don't got all night to sit around waitin' on you to make up your inebriated mind, so what's it gonna be?"

"Just hold on a minute." Looking decidedly less high, he straightened. "Let me see if I got this straight. After shooting your dad's motorcycle gang members and stealing their bikes, you want to sell me one?" His voice raised two whole octaves. "Do I look suicidal? Where am I gonna fence a stolen Lone Coaster's bike around here?"

"Did I say it belonged to an LC?" I glanced at Tarq. "I don't remember sayin' that. Did I say that?" I looked back at Rooney. "And who said anythin' about shootin' anyone?"

It was Rooney's turn to throw his hands up. "Your dad is who! He came into the gas station, and as one of his biker bitches grabbed me around the throat and dragged me over the counter, strangling me, he *smiled at me*. He said if I didn't tell him exactly where you were, he was going to gut me and use my entrails to hang me up by my balls and watch while vultures pecked my eyeballs out. *Who says that, Shaila?*"

"Stone Hawkins is who." I wasn't impressed. I'd seen and heard it all before. "But what's that got to do with capitalism? You want the bike or not?"

"*Jesus Christ.*" He rubbed a hand over his face. "You're as cold as him."

"I'll be a lot colder when I'm livin' in Kentucky away from this heat."

"Stop telling me where you're going!" He pulled the neck of his shirt aside. "I still got the marks where I was strangled today because of you, and I didn't even know anything then!"

"Well, now you know I got a bike. Want it?"

"Are you not listening to me?" Rooney yelled.

I reached over and pulled the dingy curtain aside on the only window facing the back of his trailer. "Did I mention I have a small armory in the saddle bags?"

"I'm not buying that, that...." Rooney glanced out the window and his mouth dropped.

I smiled sweetly. "Pretty, ain't she?"

"*Shit*," Rooney whispered.

I tried to sweeten the deal so we could get out of here sooner rather than later. "You don't even have to fence it around here. She rides like a dream. Drive her to the west coast. Heck, get out of state. Drive to Washington. Keep goin'. I hear Canada's pretty. This bike's got plenty of miles in her. You could go anywhere."

"I can't afford that." Rooney glanced at Tarq, then his gaze landed on me. "Even at a dead biker discount."

I slapped him on the shoulder. "Then it's a good thing we're friends, because I'm gonna give you one helluva discount." I leveled him with a look that said I meant business. "How much cash you got?"

"Five, maybe six hundred bucks."

A couple hundred more than I was expecting, but a couple thousand less than I wanted. No other options, I took it. "Six hundred and you got a deal."

Rooney rubbed his chin as he looked out the window again. "Whose was it?"

"Can't say I caught his name." Technically, it wasn't a lie.

"Someone from around here?"

I had to give Rooney credit. For all the years I'd worked with him at the gas station, I never took him for more than a mind-altered stoner who didn't have a whole lot going on upstairs, but this Rooney here was holding his own. "To my knowledge, no, it wasn't someone from around here."

Rooney frowned. "Rival MC to your Dad's?"

"I don't know if I would say that." After all, Rush was gonna make me his old lady.

Rooney snorted. "Well, if the dude who was driving this is found dead in LC territory, it won't be long before it's a rival gang."

I inwardly cringed at his all-too-real assessment, but there was nothing I could do about it now. I wasn't sorry those jerks who were gonna shoot us were dead. I just didn't want to be the source of some all-out biker war. "All the more reason to make a decision quick and do what you're gonna do with the bike."

"Fine. I'll take it." Rooney looked at me, and for the first time in all the while I'd known him, he looked un-stoned. Well, more like kinda green and kinda sick and a whole lot resigned, but not high. "If I get dead because of this, I'm coming back to haunt you." He glanced at Tarq. "And you too."

In his ever-present hold on honesty, my man laid out the truth for Rooney. "There is no such thing as ghosts."

Rooney flinched at the deep quiet of Tarquin's voice, but he didn't back off. "There will be if I get dead because of her." Pushing past both of us, he moved toward the one bedroom at the back of the trailer. "Wait there."

Tarq watched Rooney disappear down the short hall. Then he turned to me and lowered his voice. "I do not like this."

"Yeah?" Me either. Something felt off all of a sudden.

But I didn't connect the dots to that off feeling and Rooney's missing cell phone until it was too late.

Chapter
NINETEEN

Tarquin

THE DIRTY-HAIRED DRUG ADDICT CAME OUT OF THE SLEEPING quarters with a cell phone to his ear and a gun drawn. His arm shaking, he pointed the weapon at us.

"Yeah," he said into the phone. "I got them right here."

My gun already in my left hand, I gave him one warning as I slowly palmed my knife. "Hang up if you want to live."

"Tarq," my woman whispered. "Find out who he's talkin' to first. Don't kill him."

"If he intends to kill us, I make no promises." I raised my voice. "Hang up. Now."

Extending his arm further, the addict's hand shook worse. "No way. I hang up and you'll do something to me."

My woman put her hands on her hips. "Like what? Sell you a bike?" She shook her head. "You're a dumbshit, Rooney." She glanced at me. "Let's go. He won't shoot. He's got no balls." She made to move past me.

In a calculated maneuver to safeguard, I stepped in front of her.

"Hey!" The addict waved the gun. "One more move and I shoot!"

I threw my knife.

The addict screamed. Dropping his gun and his phone, he grabbed the arm my knife was embedded in and fell to his knees.

I did not hesitate. Kicking his gun aside, I pressed my 9mm to his temple as I stomped on his cell phone. "Do you know the only reason you are still alive?"

He did not answer. He cried. Like a baby.

My woman snorted. "You really are a dumbshit, Rooney. You're alive because I told him not to kill you. Tell me who you were talkin' to and you'll stay alive."

"Jesus fucking Christ, Shaila!"

"Who were you talkin' to?" she yelled.

"Your dad's driver, okay?" His body shook in pain. "Now get the fucking knife out!"

My woman didn't concede. "Where were they?" she demanded.

"I don't know," he cried.

"Not good enough," my woman snapped.

"I don't know, okay! They were here an hour ago, more, I don't know! Help me and get the fucking knife out!" He looked at the knife and cried harder.

"You're lucky I liked you, Rooney. But for the record? Now I don't." My woman fisted my knife and yanked it out.

The addict howled in pain as he fell forward.

Grabbing him by the shirt, my woman jerked him back up to his knees and wiped the blade on his clothing. "Where's the six hundred bucks? And don't mess with me, you shithead, or I'll make sure you get a matching scar on your other arm."

"Oh my God," he wailed, holding his wound. "You're fucking fucked-up, Shaila, you know that?"

"Money," she demanded of him. "NOW."

"Bedroom," he yelled back, curling in on himself. "The fucking dresser, you crazy bitch!"

I hit him.

He fell to the floor, unconscious.

"You pistol-whipped him," my woman stated, staring down at him for a moment before looking up at me.

"He called you a name. We need to go."

She kept staring at me. "No one's ever defended me like that. I mean, I get the whole thing back at the house and in the orchard, that was life or death, but this?" She shook her head. "This is different."

I did not see it as different. "We are out of time."

"You care about me."

"Woman," I warned.

"Right." She nodded. Then her gaze dropped, and she nodded again. "Okay. Let me grab the money." Inhaling, she turned toward the bedroom, but then she paused and held my knife out to me. "Here."

I took the gold-plated switchblade that had a dozen small diamonds embedded in the handle. "We do not need the money."

"Just a sec, just give me a second," she called over her shoulder as she walked into the bedroom.

"We have to leave." I looked out the front window. No headlights, no vehicles, no one on foot that I could see, but my instinct was telling me her father was close.

Drawers banged open. "I got it." She emerged from the bedroom with a handful of clothing as she shoved something into her front jeans pocket. "Let's go."

"Wait." I stepped out of the trailer. Inhaling air not rank with drugs and filth, I scanned the surrounding area. Seeing no one, I nodded at her.

She glanced nervously down the road we had come in on. "Maybe we should take the Road King if my daddy's comin'. It'll be quicker."

"Leave it." Grasping her arm, I steered her toward the shadows at the edge of the property.

She did not pull out of my grip, but she paused. "Wait. I got a bad feelin' about this. The other bike is over a mile away where we hid it, and if Daddy's close, it'll take too long to get to it. We should just take the Road King and get out of here. I'll even give Rooney his money back."

"We are not going back, and we are not stopping. They will not look for us on foot. They will expect us to be on the motorcycles we stole."

"I think Daddy'll know if we're hoofin' it," she argued. "You can hear those pipes a mile away. If he stops to listen and doesn't hear them, he'll figure it out."

I did not have time to counter.

A large vehicle came speeding down the road toward the property.

Chapter

TWENTY

Shaila

DADDY'S SUV CAME BARRELING DOWN THE ROAD AND skidded to a stop right in front of Rooney's trailer. Panic froze me in my tracks, and I whispered, "Shit."

Tarq yanked me down behind a patch of palmettos. His gun drawn, he moved in front of me just like he did in the trailer, but this time he aimed his gun.

Sparing me a glance, he put a finger to his lips.

Everything suddenly too real, fear choked my throat and I nodded.

The driver, front passenger, and one of the back doors of the SUV all opened at once.

Gun drawn, Daddy's driver strode toward the steps of the trailer.

Holding a gun himself, but not aiming it, Daddy followed his driver, and the third man followed him. But instead of stepping inside the trailer, Daddy stopped and looked right in our direction.

Already on my belly, my stomach still went south. I was sure Daddy couldn't see me, but our eyes met just the same, and in that moment, I didn't see my father.

I saw Stone Hawkins for who he really was.

A ruthless man who would sell his daughter and kill without remorse.

I glanced at the man lying next to me.

Perfectly still, his aim on the president of the Lone Coasters MC, Tarquin's finger rested on the trigger.

One shot.

One bullet and my daddy would be dead.

A pang of feelings I didn't think I'd feel hit my chest, and my heart broke. It broke for all the times the cruel man standing on that dilapidated trailer step had been an actual daddy to me—the Harley rides, the ice creams, the shoulder pats, the smiles. I remembered all of it, all at once.

But what I didn't remember was hugs, bedtime stories, or late night tuck-ins after nightmares. I didn't remember being driven to or picked up from school or sitting across a dining table over a meal with him and Mama. I didn't remember strong arms holding me if I fell, and I didn't remember a steady voice when I needed reason.

Because none of that had ever happened.

I wasn't a daughter to Stone Hawkins.

I was never anything to him but a pawn.

A pretty piece he maneuvered and groomed so he could one day use me to make a move to his advantage.

I didn't even know if the man ever loved me.

But the man lying down in the dirt beside me, ready to pull the trigger, I knew how he felt about me.

Tarquin Scott may never tell me he loved me, but he showed it.

He'd been showing it.

Ever since he said I would be his wife.

And that right there was more than the man who'd raised me had ever given me.

My breath in my throat, my heart pounding in fear, all I had to do was whisper one word.

Shoot.

But I didn't.

I couldn't.

And in the next breath, the split-second opportunity to make all of this go away vanished as swiftly as it'd appeared.

Daddy stepped into the trailer and the man behind him followed.

"Now," Tarquin whispered, grabbing my arm and quickly getting up.

Scrambling to my feet, holding the jeans I'd stolen from Rooney for Tarq, I kept bent at the waist.

My man pushed me forward with a single command. "Hurry."

We ran into the dense overgrowth and slash pines.

Palmettos whipping at my arms, spiderwebs hitting my face, I didn't stop.

I kept moving, and Tarquin kept right behind me, protecting my back.

A few paces in, a distinctive sound cracked through the forest.

Two gunshots.

A quick double tap, the sound hardly muffled by an ancient trailer shell.

My body froze, and I looked back.

The light from the trailer window barely visible through the now dense overgrowth of wild Florida woods left untamed, I heard, more than saw, the rusty metal door swing open and three men walk out.

Then, just like on a lake, voices carried through the trees.

"Which way, boss?"

"North," Daddy clipped as he and the two other men got in the SUV. "They're heading to Kentucky on a white Road King."

The SUV's doors slammed shut, and the engine whined as the driver backed out too fast in reverse.

Rooney was dead.

The only friend I'd ever had, shot twice and killed after getting stabbed and pistol-whipped... because of me.

Rooney was dead because of me.

Tears welled and slid down my cheeks as a strong hand wrapped around my arm.

Then a deep voice quietly spoke in my ear. "Let us go."

Chapter
TWENTY-ONE

Tarquin

SHE DID NOT SPEAK. For several kilometers, we pushed our way through scrub brush, palmettos and young saplings. When the threat was no longer at our backs, I took the lead. Yet she still did not utter a word as we hiked back to the other motorcycle.

I could feel her grief the same as I could taste my own thirst. With every inhale, we breathed in mulching vegetation and rot, but with every step she succumbed further to her sorrow.

When we cleared the trees and our motorcycle lay ahead under a pile of cut fronds, I stopped and turned to her.

"The addict's death was not your fault." She had asked me not to kill him. I knew she was mourning his death.

The clothing still in her arms, she looked around as if seeing the surrounding land for the first time. Her lips parted, and her voice came out haunted. "I never thought I was a bad person. Not like my daddy. I always knew he wasn't no saint, but I never thought I was like him... not till tonight anyway."

"You did not pull the trigger," I reminded her.

Her eyes, wet with tears, met mine. "Didn't I?"

"No."

"Just like that?" Guilt and regret laced her tone. "None of us woulda been here if it weren't for me."

"I would not be alive if it were not for you."

"So that makes it all okay? I killed my only friend tonight, but since I saved you, my soul's redeemed? It all works out? Even Steven?"

I did not know about her soul, nor who she was referring to. "Life is for the living."

"Well, tell that to Rooney."

I was angered that she continued to speak his name. He had shown her no loyalty. "He was not living. He was squandering his freedom on drugs, and he was not bothering to procreate life." There was no way to glorify his wasted existence.

Her face contorted with anger. "Is that the measure of a man's worth? How many babies he brings into this world? Because if that's your measure, then you better get off your high horse. You ain't no better than Rooney in that regard, unless you were lyin' to me in the first place and you do have little Tarquins runnin' around River Ranch, wonderin' where their daddy is." Her emotions in a tailspin, she choked on a sob in the dark. "Did you? Did you lie to me?" Tears ran down her face.

My chest constricted, and anger surged. I did not want to see her shed tears for that addict, nor did I want to see her cry. And I definitely did not want to have my past brought to task for actions I could neither change nor be accountable for after the fact.

My jaw ticked, and I gave her the only truth I knew. "I have not ever used the term friend. I do not know its meaning from personal experience. I am not schooled nor practiced by life's experiences, but I do know that if I had the gift of your friendship, I would have never thrown it away with a phone call to the man hunting you down to sell you. That is the measure of a man. His integrity."

Sniffling, she rubbed the sleeve of her jacket under her nose. "Well, maybe you call it integrity, but what I saw back there in that trailer? I called that fear. Rooney was afraid of my daddy. More afraid of my daddy and what he'd do to him if he found out he'd helped us than he was afraid of us. So he made a decision between the gun staring him down and the gun that could stare him down. And I don't fault him for that."

"Then what do you fault him for?" Because I could not understand how she could call a man like that a friend and not see his shortcomings.

She blinked, and then she looked at me like I was losing my mind. "He's *dead*."

I was aware. "I heard the shots, same as you."

"You don't talk ill of the dead!"

Frustrated, I raised my voice like she had. "Why not?"

She threw a hand up. "Because you just don't."

"That is not an answer." Truth knew no bounds like death or emotion.

"Because it's mean, okay? It's just plain mean!"

I had no response to that.

She let out a small cry. "And now I'm just like my daddy."

I had not met her father, but I could guarantee she was not like him. "Would you have a child and sell that child for gain?" I did not wait for her answer because I already knew it. "You would not. You are not like him." Just as I was not like River Stephens.

She swiped at her face, but the fight had left her. "You mean that or are you just sayin' it to make me stop cryin'?"

"I do not say words I do not mean."

"You said there was nothin' you disliked about me." She drew in a shaky breath. "Is that still true?"

"Yes." I did not hold it against her that she had feelings for the addict. I recognized that she had been living an isolated existence that not even the women on compound had to endure. I did not fault her for the addict's shortcomings.

Her voice quieted. "What if I said I almost told you to pull the trigger back there, when Daddy was standing on Rooney's front step?"

Hating the anguish in her eyes, I cupped her face. "I would have taken the shot and thought nothing less of you."

"I'm scared," she whispered. "I'm scared of Daddy finding you, of Rush's MC finding us, of how I feel about you, of what I've become, of your past comin' after you if they find out you're alive, of all of it, but I can't change any of it."

"You are an honorable woman, we are safe right now, and I will not let anything happen to you." Those issues I could address now. Her emotions I could not control. And as for the last fear she mentioned, I needed to come clean.

Glancing behind us, then at the buried motorcycle, I brought my gaze back to hers.

For a long moment, I studied her pretty face.

Then I told her the single resolve that had kept me alive in the swamp before she found me. "One day, I am going to kill River Stephens."

Chapter
TWENTY-TWO

Shaila

Tarquin's intense gaze cut from the pile of dead palm fronds covering the bike to me.

For three whole heartbeats, he stared at me.

Then he let words out like a confession.

"One day, I am going to kill River Stephens."

Chill bumps crawled up my spine and raced across my neck.

Then shock I didn't know I could feel after a day like today spread through my mind like fear. Biting my tongue, I spoke with a careful tone. "Because he tried to kill you and threw you out?" Murder for revenge suddenly felt a whole lot different than pulling the trigger in self-defense. A whole lot different and a whole lot bad.

"Because River Stephens is a madman."

Inhaling, I grasped at reason.

I couldn't argue with his justification, but I could see a big logistical problem with it. "What'll happen to all those people at River Ranch if he suddenly up and dies?" I couldn't imagine three hundred people like Tarquin abruptly thrust into society all on their own."

His nostrils flared with an inhale. "I do not care."

It hit me so hard and fast, a freight train couldn't have had this much impact if it'd barreled into me on the spot.

Me and Tarquin Scott were the same.

The exact same.

I grew up around bikers. My daddy was the president of their club. He ruled those bikers like River Stephens ruled those River Ranch folks, and now my daddy and his bikers were coming after me like River Stephens and his people had gone after Tarq. I didn't have no loyalty from Daddy when it'd really counted, same as Tarquin had no loyalty from River or his people.

For all intents and purposes, River Stephens was Tarquin's daddy, and he'd sold him out for a flower. My daddy had sold me out for an alliance.

I didn't know which was worse.

They were both wrong.

And both of them were bad men.

I'd thought about telling Tarquin to pull the trigger when he'd had a clear shot at the man who'd made me. Was I gonna condemn Tarquin for wanting to kill the man who'd had him beaten, stabbed, and tossed out like yesterday's trash?

No, I wasn't.

But I didn't want to lose us because of that madman River Stephens or because of my daddy.

"If you get caught, it'll ruin your life." And mine, but I didn't say that.

"I will not get caught," he stated with complete confidence.

It suddenly dawned on me. "Is that why you wanna become an Army Ranger? So you can learn how to fight?"

"I know how to fight."

I didn't argue, because he was right. Instead, I kept quiet and waited. There was more to it than he was letting on, but I knew enough about him to know that asking wouldn't get me answers. The only way I would find out what was in his head was if he decided to tell me.

So I stood there.

The cicadas sang their nightly song. The stiff palmetto fronds clapped against each other in the slight breeze. The scent of pine and moldy, dead leaves filled the air, and my man held my cheek and stared past me.

Then his almost colorless blue-eyed gaze met me in the moonlight, and his deep voice filled the space around us. But it wasn't melodic. He didn't talk like the slick humidity coating the palmettos in a layer of moisture. And he didn't speak like he was the hot sun beating down on your back, making you feel his presence long after he'd gone.

No, Tarquin Scott spoke like he was the dirt beneath your feet. Dark, rich, and heavy, his voice coated everything around you and grounded you to the very earth you were standing on. You felt his pull in every one of your leg muscles as if he were holding you down like gravity.

Because that was what Tarquin Scott was—deep, dark, soil of the earth *gravity*.

"There was a brother on compound," he quietly stated with no more or no less emotion than a summer breeze in the Glades. "He had been in the military. Army Ranger." His throat moved with a swallow. His eyes scanned the woods. "When my birth mother was killed, after I buried her, he came to me and told me an address. He said to memorize it. I did not question him. Strong, silent, he was the best shot on compound. Every female sought his attention. His eyes were haunted, but his actions were just, and I respected him." Tarquin glanced at me. "I did as he said."

Biting the inside of my cheek, I nodded.

His gaze drifted again as his thumb absently stroked my cheek. "That night he told me to never forget the address. Then he did not speak of it again. For many turns around the sun, I did not question the significance. I merely repeated the address in my own thoughts. I did it so often, the street name and number became more sacred than scripture." His chest rose with an inhale. "When I had been beaten for the last time and my flesh pierced with metal, the pain was so great, I wanted to succumb to it. But then I heard his voice, and he placed his knife in my hand. He said, *Of their own accord, Rangers lead the way. Do not be weak, Tarquin. Remember the address.*"

I put two and two together. "The address is for an Army recruiter's office."

He nodded once. "I do not want to learn how to fight."

Alarm whispered across my consciousness. "You don't?"

"No." His lethal gaze met mine. "I want to learn how to kill."

Oh dear Lord of mercy. "You already know how to do that," I whispered.

"Not well enough to defeat River Stephens."

"And after?" I dared to ask. "After you... defeat him?"

"I live."

"How?" Would he have peace then?

"With you."

Sweet Jesus, my breath caught in my lungs, but I kept on. "Peacefully?"

He nodded once.

"Will that be enough?" Would I be enough?

He did not hesitate. "Yes."

My anxiety came down a notch, but I needed more. I needed answers, and suddenly I needed a plan. Something to look forward to. Something to work toward. Something to focus on other than this day and this night. "And after the Army? What will you do?"

"Anything not involving digging."

I glanced at the bike hidden under the branches and furiously thought. Because I wasn't the only one who needed a plan. He did too. He needed something to focus on, something more than righting the wrongs of his past. He needed a future to look forward to as well. "You like riding. You could be a mechanic. Work on bikes?"

His tone darkened with warning. "Are you finished?"

"I..." The rest of my response caught on the sudden dryness in my throat, and oh my stars, he was intimidating. And beautiful. And more man than any one male I had ever met. "I don't know what you mean."

The darkened warning in his tone, his eyes, it turned into something else. Something I hadn't seen since owls were above our heads and he was inside me.

"Do not ever attempt to tend to me again." His tender

hold on my cheek became a firm grasp of my chin. "I do not need it, and I do not desire it."

My skin tingled, my core pulsed like a starved animal, and my body ached for him as my voice shook. "Then what do you desire?"

"You. *Only* you."

His mouth slammed over mine.

For the first time in my life, I tasted true need.

Chapter
TWENTY-THREE

Tarquin

THE BLACK MOTORCYCLE WAS AT THE BOTTOM OF A POND.

Our long hike through the dark was behind us.

The cabin stood before us.

But as I stared at the rotting structure, I knew the true test lay before us.

With her shotgun perched on her shoulder and the pants she had taken in one arm, she opened a padlock on the outside of the door to the cabin.

Without seeing the inside, I knew we could not live here long.

Roughhewn wood, no insulation, sagging roof, no foundation, not raised off the ground but one step—the cabin would not survive the elements for long.

She pushed the door open, and the scent of must and mold followed.

"Let me just find a light." She took a step forward.

I stopped her with a hand on her arm. "Do not turn a light on." I could not be sure we had not been followed.

She looked over her shoulder. "You think we were tracked all the way out here?"

I did not know. I had never been trained as a hunter. I had relied on instinct getting out here, but the loud call of the cicadas had masked most sounds, and once we were deep in the cover of the mangroves and pines, I did not have enough moonlight to see behind us. "Can you make your way around the cabin without light?"

She swatted at a mosquito. "Yeah."

"Inside," I ordered.

She stepped in, and I followed. Closing the door behind me, I dropped the two backpacks to the floor. "Does it lock from the inside?" I could not see anything in the pitch dark.

"Yes." She reached around me, and I heard her secure the padlock from outside to the inside of the door.

The air still, sweat pricked at my neck. "Are there any screened windows?"

"There's one, and I got a fit-in screen for it. You know, one of those things you can get at the hardware store."

I did not know. "Where is it?"

"I'll get it."

The air shifted as she moved around me, then moonlight filtered in as she pushed a dark curtain aside. The sound of wood sliding against wood broke the silence, and a moment later, I could smell the scent of swamp, mangroves and pine that was as familiar to me as breathing.

Pushing the window halfway up and fitting a wood-framed screen into the casement, she then closed the window enough to secure the frame into place. "There we go." Brushing her hands off, she stepped back.

I assessed the cabin in the light from the moon. One small cot, one small table with two small chairs, an arm's length of counter fastened to the exposed wood wall—the entire space was maybe two by three paces, and it was filled with supplies. Canned goods, paper goods, bottled water, lanterns, blankets, and books.

"What do you think?" she asked hesitantly.

Despite her supplies, I thought she had far underestimated her food resources. We would not last until summer on what she had stocked. "Do you have cooking fuel?" A daily fire would be difficult during summer rains.

"Yep. I got a campin' stove that runs on these little tanks, and I got two cases of 'em. I think I thought of everythin'—water, food, lanterns, batteries. And I got a solar shower."

"Solar shower?"

"Yeah, you hang the bag up where it can get sunshine and fill it with water, and presto, by the end of the day, the sun heats the water for you. All I gotta do is clear a few tree branches, and we should get enough direct sunlight."

Only on days the sun shone. But I did not comment. I also did not comment on the sleeping cot sized for one. I would fashion a larger frame from the slash pines and hopefully she had another mattress of air we could use.

She crossed her arms, and her voice quieted. "You're not sayin' anythin'."

"Take the sleeping cot." I turned a chair toward the window. "I will keep watch until daybreak."

She did not respond.

Neither did she move.

She stood there, her gaze assessing her supplies.

Then her shoulders slumped and she exhaled. "Okay, look, I know this ain't the Taj Mahal of accommodations. And I got no idea what kinda life you been used to or what those men's quarters were like that you talked about, but this is what we got. It ain't half bad compared to sleepin' out in the open, and it's a hell of a lot better than bein' dead."

I did not know what the Taj Mahal was, but I did not disagree. I took two bottles of water from a stack on the ground and handed her one. "Drink."

She took the water. "You can't just do that all the time, you know, and get away with it."

I opened the water and drank the entire bottle. "Get away with what?" Her bottled water supply would not last us a fortnight. We would have to boil water from the well outside to have safe drinking water.

"Bossin' me around and not sayin' what's on your mind."

I studied her a moment.

I could not think of a single female at River ranch who would have exhibited the type of strength and fortitude she had shown today. Neither could I think of any men, save for the hunters or the brother who had made me memorize the address of the place where I could become an Army Ranger, who would have come out of today's events unscathed.

My woman was not weak.

She deserved the truth of my thoughts.

I replaced the cap on the empty water bottle and set it on the small table. "Your food rations will not last till summer. Your water supply will not last more than a fortnight. The cabin does not have any means for proper air circulation, and it is not suitable for long-term habitation. We will not be comfortable come summer, nor will we be safe here during the hurricane months. The roof will not bear its own weight for long, and the bed is too small."

"Huh." Crossing her arms, she sat on the cot and dropped her gaze. "I didn't think much about hurricanes. One hasn't come through these parts in a while." She looked up at me. "What'd you do at River Ranch when there was one?"

"We covered all the windows with sheets of wood, brought everything inside we could, and everyone moved into the concrete-reinforced structure we had on compound for the duration of the storm."

In the barely penetrating light of the moon, I saw her eyebrows draw together. "What structure was that?"

"The main hall."

"You had an event hall?"

"It was a large building that had seating for everyone and a kitchen where the women prepared food. It was used for gatherings, worship and meals." I did not want to think about River Ranch any more than I wanted to think about what the next few fortnights in this cabin would be like as I conditioned my body. I needed to be stronger than before I was vanquished so I would be ready for the Army Rangers.

"So it had electricity and plumbin'?" she asked, continuing her inquiry.

I nodded once, trying to remember any words the brother from River Ranch had spoken about being an Army Ranger, but I could recall none save for the fact that he had been one.

"Oh. Well." She slapped her hands on her thighs and

stood. "Guess that settles that. Sounds nicer than here for sure." Reaching over a stacked pile of canned goods, she grabbed a blanket and sat back down on the cot. Kicking off her boots, she brought her legs up, and despite the heat inside the cabin, she shook out the blanket and laid it over herself.

Then she turned her back on me and clipped out words in anger. "Night night, sleep tight, don't let the bed bugs bite, and whatever the hell else you say to someone before you fall asleep."

I removed my gun from my back waistband and placed it on the table. The chair creaked with my weight, and the table wobbled from either uneven supports or flooring or both.

Stretching my legs out in front of me, I glanced out the window at the moonlight filtering through the slash pines, and my stomach made a sound of hunger.

"Great," she said with attitude. "I can't turn on a light to get some food, but I gotta listen to that all night?"

"We will eat come daybreak." It was not only the light I was concerned about, but the scent of food. With no perimeter to stop wildlife, the scent of cooking could draw any number of animals to our doorstep.

"Terrific," she sulked.

I thought about what she had said earlier. "Why would I want to leave the Army?" She had said they provided housing. It had to be better than this.

Rolling over, she stared at me. "Are you serious?"

"Yes."

She sighed as if irritated. "You don't go into the military without risk. No one does. They send men to war. Yeah, it's all in the name of protectin' our country, and I respect that, a whole lot, but that don't mean it's not dangerous as hell. That kinda life ain't no better than the club life my daddy lives, and you saw how that turned out today." Her voice quieted. "I don't wanna live that kinda life, Tarquin. Wonderin' every time you step out the door if you're comin' back." She stared at me. "I want to be with you, not be a widow."

I nodded once as if I understood.

"You know if you sign up, you only gotta give them eight years, and I don't think all of that is even servin', or active duty, as they call it. I think you can give them half that, or six years, and then be like, on reserve."

"Reserve?"

"Yeah, like standby, in case they need more soldiers or somethin' for some emergency. You could do that. Go in, serve your time, get out, then start another career. That's why I mentioned workin' on bikes. You could do that. We could have a little house. Maybe by the ocean." Her voice turned quiet. "We could have our own family."

Since the first assault to my flesh from my compound brothers, I was driven solely by one thought. I wanted River Stephens dead. But I knew I could not breach the compound and do it myself knowing only the skills of a digger. I wanted to become an Army Ranger to learn the skills necessary to take down River Stephens.

It had been my only plan.

But sitting in the dark with my woman, the seed of a new thought took hold and I could almost taste it.

The possibility of a different life.

A life I had had no concept of before this moment.

A free life. With my woman. In a house by the sea.

Her body swollen with my offspring. And as I looked at my beautiful woman, a night breeze blew in the scent of the Everglades, and I wanted the life she described. "I have never seen the ocean."

A smile, pure of heart and full of hope, spread across her face. "Well, Tarquin Scott, I think it's time we fixed that."

Lightning lit up the night a moment before thunder clapped, then the sky opened up. A sudden torrent of rain hit the small cabin and all sound save for the weather was drowned out.

My woman lifted the blanket in invitation. "Lie with me?"

I glanced out the window.

No one would come this deep in to the Glades in this weather.

I removed my boots and stood.

Chapter
TWENTY-FOUR

Tarquin

THE SMALL CABIN FILLED WITH HER FEMININE VOICE AS WORDS tumbled out of her mouth. For four fortnights every morning had begun like this—with my woman singing. And I had listened to every word that had crossed her lips.

But this morning, I was not hearing the individual words of the song.

The sun just up, heat filling the small enclosed space, I was fighting off agitation. "What are you doing?" It was too early for this.

Her hips moved from side to side as if she were being taken. "What's it sound like, silly? I'm singin'."

She was not only singing.

Gritting my teeth, sitting at the small table in the middle of the cabin, I whittled at the piece of wood in my hand. My cock hardening, my jaw ticked. I had already taken her when we awoke. I had also taken her before we had bedded down last night.

Holding a cooking utensil, she spun around and leaned down toward me. Her sleeveless, tight shirt doing nothing to hide the sway of her breasts, she sang out words to a song I had never heard.

Because I had never heard any songs.

Except the ones she sang.

Every day.

For the past two months.

Music had never been allowed on compound. I had been used to nothing except the sound of the Glades around me. But for eight weeks I had been listening to her voice bend and shape words, and I had thought about the mostly senseless lyrics late in the evenings, long after she had stopped singing for the day. I even compared the range of her voice against the natural sounds of the Glades.

I did not know if I hated her singing or anticipated it.

All I knew, the more I took her, the more she sang.

But today, the hip swaying was new.

I did not like it.

I did not like it at all.

"Finish breakfast," I clipped, unable to stop the thought that if she were on compound, she would be taken by all the men. They would all desire her. The thought was not new. I had had it with increasing frequency the more days we spent out here. I did not like the thought any more than I could control it surfacing.

Dismissing it and her hip sway, I used my knife to carve the next angle into the small piece of wood in my hand.

She laughed a laugh that was not of humor but mockery. "Who pissed in your Cheerios this morning?"

Pissed? Cheerios? "Watch your mouth." The thought of her mouth being desired by the brothers on compound surfaced, and I had to remind myself I was not River Ranch and never would be again. I would take my own life before I allowed that. Hers too, if it came to it.

She laughed. "Or you'll what? Bend me over your knee?" Her voice lowered as she taunted me. "Kiss me?"

Dropping the wood and my knife, I stood.

Her smile disappeared, and her throat moved with a swallow, but the attitude did not leave her. "Someone's in a mood today."

I was in no kind of mood. "I do not have moods." I had a disposition, and it was singular. "Take your underwear off." I hated them and the word.

"Ha! Nice try. You already had your mornin' allotment." She waved the cooking utensil at me. "Now I'm cookin' because I'm hungry."

Precise and quick, my movements practiced, I grabbed the material as it hugged her hips, but this time I did not drag it down her thighs. I fisted my hands and yanked.

The material tore.

"Tarquin!" she gasped, her hands going to my shoulders and her fingers digging into my flesh. Her grip signaling intent, not protest, she leaned in to me. "Those were my nice lace panties. They matched the bra."

"You will no longer wear such undergarments." I hated how they withheld access to what was mine. "Spread your legs."

"So romantic." Layering sarcasm with obedience, she sat on the edge of the bed and spread her legs, but her shirt fell between her thighs and covered the view I wanted most. Her voice sweet, she pushed at my patience with words meant to provoke. "You got nothin' to say for yourself about my pretty underwear you ruined?"

My cock already desperate for her, I turned off the camping stove and shoved my pants down before fisting myself. I did not think about how she had become an addiction I could not fight. "Lift your shirt."

She fingered the hem like this was a game she wanted to play until sunset. "How far?"

If she was an addiction I could not fight, her strong will was the drug I could not quit. "Show me your cunt." I wanted to see her desire for me.

Her voice dropped. "And you'll what?" She slowly lifted her shirt past her curved hips. A smile teasing her lips, her finger skirted the edge of her womanhood. "Play with me?"

"I do not play games." Staring at the wetness dripping out of her cunt onto her soft thigh, I stroked myself.

"Maybe I want you to play one with me."

I was not playing at anything. "I will fuck you, and you will come before I release my seed deep inside your cunt."

She shoved a finger inside herself.

My nostrils flared, and I bit out a command in warning, "Stop."

"Why?" She stroked into herself. "Are you the only one who can touch me like this?"

"Yes." I had fought for my rights to her, and I had won. We had been out here two months, and I had trained my body every day and tended to her body every sunup and sundown. I owned her cunt, I owned her orgasms, and I owned her body. She was mine. "Remove your finger or I will do it for you."

Half breathless, half defiant, her voice lowered. "You make me crazy."

She made me weak. Which was more dangerous than living out here without the protection of a guarded compound around us.

Pushing her to her back, I brought my cock to her entrance and gave fair warning. "I own your releases. I tend to you. I make you come."

"Yes, you do," she whispered with a coy smile on her face.

I shoved into her.

Her mouth opened, her back arched, and she let a sound she only made when my cock was inside her. Deeper, throatier, the moan was more than when my fingers took her cunt or my mouth sucked her clit.

I liked this sound better.

I was addicted to this sound.

"Again," I demanded, pulling back and trusting hard.

But she did not make the sound of need again. She bit her lip, cupped my cheek, and her darkened eyes met mine. "Kiss me," she whispered.

Except she did not merely whisper it.

She begged for it.

She begged for it like she needed it, asking for more as if I were not enough. As if my cock was not already deep inside her cunt, driving her toward a release.

Anger surged.

I did not kiss. I fucked. She liked it. She had always liked it.

"Take what I am giving you." I ground the words as I thrust into her hard.

Her smile disappeared, her hand dropped, and she turned her head.

My jaw clenched, I held her hips down. "Speak."

"Why?" she defied. "You don't seem to need my input for this."

My cock deep inside her, harboring anger at her words I did not fully understand, I needed to release, and so did she. "You will come," I ordered.

"Yes, sir," she replied dryly.

My hands fisted, my nostrils flared, and I jerked back. Pulling out of her, I shoved off the makeshift bed I had fashioned from slash pine boughs, hitched my pants and stormed out of the cabin, slamming the door behind me.

The mosquitoes hitting my flesh before the heat of the humidity, I picked up the ax she had brought to the cabin as part of her supplies, and I wielded it.

"So that's it?" The cabin door banged open behind me. "I don't get to ask for you to kiss me or anythin' else I want and you get to storm off like a spoiled brat?"

I swung the ax.

Metal met pine.

Splinters flew.

Raising her voice, she spat anger at me. "I'm talkin' to you."

Yanking the ax from the wood, saying nothing, I swung again.

"Fine! Don't talk to me. Do your stupid, *stupid* silent, dumbass treatment. I don't need you anyway. I never did!"

I swung the ax into the wood, let go of the handle and spun. "What is wrong with the way I take you?" I roared.

"*Take me?*" Her voice pitching high, she looked at me as if I were the insane one. "We're back to that load of crap again? Take me, make me, break me." Rattling off the words in quick succession, she threw her hands up. "I give up. You ain't never gonna talk normal or *be* normal, so forget it. All you do is run in the woods, swing that ax and grow your muscles when you're not fuckin' me. And, yes, I said fuckin', because that's what you do." Her eyes welled. "But forget it. Forget I said a damn thing." She stormed back into the cabin.

Chest heaving, anger hotter than the air, I stood there.

My cock was covered with the cream of her cunt, and my jeans were sticking to my sex. I wanted to release inside her tightness as much as I wanted to pin her down and withhold satisfaction from her.

Unaccustomed to females talking back, despising the pressure in my chest every time she was upset, I pressed for a solution that did not entail holding her down and fucking her, but I thought of none.

Because the more I contemplated restraining her, the more my cock throbbed for release.

I did not want to kiss her.

I did not want to hear her sing.

I did not want her breasts provocatively swaying in my face like she was asking for more attention than I was giving her.

I wanted to fuck her hard.

She was mine.

I had earned rights to her.

I could do as I pleased.

Breath short, fists clenched, I strode to the cabin, took the one step up and threw the door open.

With her back to me as she tended the hot plate, she jumped, but she did not turn around. "Close the damn door. All this in and out is doin' nothin' but givin' those damn mosquitoes a free-for-all."

I did not move.

"I said, *shut the door.*" She turned. Cooking utensil in hand, eyes wet from tears, anger contorted her face. "You want us to die from West Nile vi—"

I slammed the door shut. "Turn off the burner."

"Take your attitude somewhere else. I'm makin' breakfast." She turned her back on me.

Grabbing her wrist with one hand, I reached around her with the other and turned the camp stove off for the second time. "Do you want my hands on you?" Jaw tight, I ground the question out.

She did not answer.

I raised my voice. "Do you?"

"Screw you."

"Do. You. Want. My. Hands. On. You?"

"Yes!"

I gripped the back of her neck, spun her and pushed her down to the table. Holding her there with one hand on her nape, the other still gripping her wrist, I leaned over her back. "Do you want to be kissed?" I kicked her legs apart. "Or do you want to be fucked?" Because she was not getting both. Not now.

Breathing hard, her mouth open, she did not speak.

I shoved her tight shirt up and slapped her bare ass. "Answer me!"

Jerking from shock, she dropped the cooking utensil and gripped the edge of the table with her free hand. "So this is the real you? This is the *real* Tarquin Scott? You like to get all rough on a woman?" Words meant to inflame flew from her mouth. "Is that want you did at that sick compound of yours?"

"*Answer my question,*" I growled, my anger ratcheting.

She defied me. "No."

I slapped her ass again. "ANSWER."

"Figure it out!"

Releasing her wrist, I stood to my full height and yanked my jeans down. Chest heaving, expecting her to fight, wondering if she would kick me, I waited.

But she did not get up.

She did not make a move to leave.

She gripped the other side of the table.

Taking her action as consent, I kicked her legs wider and stroked myself. Then my gaze caught an open container on the shelf.

Still holding her down, I reached over and dug two fingers through the cooking lard.

I brought them to her anus. "Last chance," I warned.

Her mouth gasped, her voice hitched, but her cunt dripped. "Screw you, Tarquin Scott."

I shoved a finger into her ass.

"*Ahhh.*" Her body jerked, and she strained against my hold on her neck. "What the hell are you doin'?"

I worked the grease in then shoved a second finger inside. "Give me an answer."

"Wait!" Her hands fisted, and she pounded them on the table. "*Wait.*"

She had defied me, so I defied her. "No." I stroked deep into her ass and repeated my question. "Fucked or kissed? Make a decision or tell me to stop," I demanded.

Her breath hitched, and she let out a half moan, half growl, but she did not tell me to stop. "I asked...," she panted. "*What. Are you doin'?*"

The grease warm, my fingers eased in and out even though she clenched at my invasion. "Fucking you or kissing you. Decide," I ordered.

Saying nothing, she made little more than a sound that was half grunt, half groan.

"NOW."

"Kissin'," she ground out. "*Kissing.*"

I dropped to one knee and latched onto her clit as I drove my greased fingers deep.

Slamming her cunt into my face, her back arched, and she came off the table. The cry of a desperate animal ripped from her lungs, and she fucked my face.

I fucked her ass with my fingers.

The hole of her cunt started to pulse around nothing.

I pushed her back down to the table.

She shoved her needy cunt against my tongue.

I probed her twice then abruptly stood and withdrew my fingers. "I am taking your ass."

On the verge of coming, she begged. "Oh God, oh God, *please.*" On tiptoe, her ass in the air, she gripped the table for leverage and pushed against my thighs.

I shoved the head of my cock into her.

Her cry filled the cabin, my eyes rolled back in my head, then my cock had a mind of its own.

No control, I thrust into her anus to the hilt.

"Oh shit!" she cried through a groan. *"I'm comin'."*

Tight.

Hot.

Greased.

Fuck.

Pounding into her, my hips pumped three times, and I was releasing.

Coming.

Roaring.

No control.

Filling her forbidden entrance.

Sullying her.

Ruining her.

Breaking.

I jerked out and shoved into her cunt.

"AHHHH, Tarquin!"

The last of my seed pumped into her pulsing cunt, but I didn't stop.

Hands gripping her waist, hips thrusting, cock raw, I fucked her.

And fucked her.

And fucked her.

Her anus leaked the act of my defilement.

Her thighs banged against the table with my every thrust.

Her cunt started to constrict again.

My head spinning, my mind shamed, our bodies dripping sweat—I drove forward.

Faster, deeper.

With the sound of sex permeating every corner of the cabin, my balls drew tight.

Jerking out and spinning her, I lifted her to the table and shoved her legs up. Her back hit the hard surface, she spread her thighs wide, and I drove back into her.

Then I fucked her harder.

Unmerciful, uncontrolled, my strength slapping against her softness, I fucked her hard.

Her body reacted.

Nipples peaked, mouth open, groans coming out of her unlike any I had ever heard from a female, her cunt gripped tight with the first spasm of her release.

I slammed my mouth over hers.

My cock fucking her cunt with skill, I came deep inside her pussy as my mouth took hers with no finesse.

Chapter
TWENTY-FIVE

Shaila

H IS MOUTH CRUSHED MINE WITH THE FORCE OF A HURRICANE, and he came inside me.

He came inside me *everywhere*.

I could feel it.

Sliding out of my body from every…. Oh Jesus.

Holding on to him for dear life, I shivered.

Sweet Lord of mercy.

His tongue, the devil between his legs—God forgive me, I was a dirty, dirty woman, but praise Jesus and all that was holy, because *that* felt amazing.

I shivered again, and he yanked out of me like I was on fire.

Holding himself over me, his forehead hit my shoulder and his chest rose and fell like he'd just run clear from Mama's house.

"I don't know what you did to me," I admitted, "but I done broke." Maybe permanently. How was I supposed to come back from that? Now his cock going where the sun don't shine was all I was gonna be thinking about. That and regular sex. Because Tarquin Scott had turned me into a hussy.

Shoving off me without making eye contact, he reached for his jeans. "I did not break you." His tone rough, he turned his back on me.

Pushing up, I frowned. "Don't get me wrong, I'm not complainin'."

"You were," he accused, reaching for a T-shirt.

I looked between my legs. He was coming out of me from every dang hole. "That's because you wouldn't kiss me." Shit, sex was messy. "Hand me a washcloth." So much for not sullying the dining table. "How many times did you come anyways?"

Spinning on me, he got in my face. Then he threw the last words I was expecting at me. "I do not like to kiss."

Just like that, it was all back. Every word of our fight earlier, my hurt feelings and a whole mess of others I didn't understand. Like a damn faucet with a leak problem, my eyes welled. "What's that supposed to mean?" He didn't like me?

"I am not repeating myself." Giving me his back again, he snatched a washcloth from the shelf he'd made with his bare hands and tossed it at me.

Hurt mixed with indignation, and my attitude took a front seat. "I didn't ask you to repeat yourself. I asked what in the heck you meant. Maybe you should try explainin' yourself for once." All the residual good feelings from sex gone, I wiped myself and fought stupid tears. "Because you sure suck at that."

"I do not like kissing!" he roared.

Half naked, vulnerable and hurt, I jerked at his outburst, but then I yelled right back. "Well, I don't like yellin' at me!"

Face furious, he stared.

Tears spilling, I looked away. "Fine, whatever, I don't like kissin' you anyway. Go kiss someone else then, you stupid jerk." I shoved off the table and cursed the small cabin. Nowhere to go, I yanked my top down and gave him my bare-ass backside. Tears sliding down my face in earnest, I picked up the spatula and shoved cold hash around the pan.

"Stupid jerk?" he asked, low and controlled.

Fighting to keep my voice even, I forced words out. "If the shoe fits."

"Turn," he demanded.

"No." I couldn't help it, a sob escaped. Then, because I wasn't humiliated enough, his baby-making soldiers dripped out of my behind. "Go away."

"Turn around."

"*Leave.*" I drove the spatula across the pan like a woman possessed.

Sex, musk, bar soap, I smelled him as his body heat surrounded my back, but he didn't touch me. For three whole heartbeats, I felt him there.

Then his voice, quiet and low, touched my ear. "Are you with child?"

I burst into tears.

In a move that was as unexpected as the turn my life took two months ago, he put his arms around me.

But Tarquin Scott did not comfort.

He screwed like his life depended on it. He ate without

comment. He could fasten, make, whittle, fix or mend anything. He didn't speak unless what he had to say was important. And he never cuddled. Ever. He only held me at night, because if he didn't, one of us would fall off the wooden bed frame he'd made the first week we'd been out here. He would lock his arm around me, lay his head back, then tell me to go to sleep.

And that was it.

For a few minutes every night, after he'd made love to me, or screwed me, depending on his mood, his arm would stay locked tight around me.

It was my favorite part of every day, and I cherished it.

I cherished it more than the weekly visits Daddy would make to our house right after he moved me and Mama in.

I'd waited all week to see Daddy. He was my ounce of sanity in the days when Mama was coming off the drugs and wasn't good for nothing except crying and soiling her sheets and begging me to call Daddy so she could get high.

Daddy would come once a week during those awful months, and his smile was always accompanied with reassurances that Mama was fine, that we'd be fine, that everything would settle in, and Lord have mercy, I waited for that man to show up more than I waited for the sun to rise.

I'd never needed anybody as much as I needed Daddy back in those days.

I never even liked to need anybody.

I was Stone Hawkins's daughter, and even as a young girl, I knew what that meant. I had to be tough and strong and hold my own and never let 'em see me sweat. Weakness was a two-headed snake, and I was having none of that.

But I let weakness in when I was eight and I waited for Daddy every dang week just so I could get a hug.

And that's what every night out in the cabin in the middle of the Glades felt like.

I was waiting for my hug.

From a man who was a thousand times harder to read than my own daddy. A man who'd said he'd marry me. But also told me he didn't want to kiss me. And who was now holding me tight, with his arms locked around me like he cared about the very feelings he was in part to blame for putting there.

God help me, I didn't know if I could do this.

Which only made me cry harder.

But Tarquin Scott didn't say one word about my tears.

No shushing, no soothing, not even a word of scolding, he just stood behind me after asking if I was carrying his child like that was something you asked a woman every dang day of her life.

"You can't just ask me that," I cried, sniffling like a baby. "You don't pick a fight and say you don't wanna kiss a woman one moment, then the very next moment hug her and ask if she's knocked up."

"I am not hugging you. I am behind you. I asked the question before I put my arms around you and more than one moment had passed."

"*Sweet Jesus*, give me patience." I pushed his arms away, and he let me. Turing to face him, I swiped at my face. "A hug's a hug, no matter how you give it. And that last part is semantics." A mess of crying tears, I was still proud of myself for using that last word that'd been one of my vocabulary words from the online high school courses I'd taken. "The point is, you don't have no right to comfort me when I'm cryin' after the mean things you said to me."

His expression carefully blank, his arms at his sides, it was his eyes that gave him away. One twitched, and I knew he was fighting for patience with me same as I was struggling to have it for him. And Lord have mercy, of all things, if that didn't make me go soft on him.

"Don't look at me like that." I pointed at him. "I'm not lettin' you off the hook."

"I am not giving you a look."

"No, you're not."

Ever so slightly, his jaw ticked as his throat moved with a swallow.

"See!" I pointed again. "That, right there. I saw it. Pretend to be calm all you want, I know what you're thinkin', and trust me, the feelin' is mutual."

"You have no idea what I am thinking."

His damn formal way of speech. "You know, you can use a dang contraction every once in a while. It wouldn't kill you."

"I do not know what a contraction is, and I do not care."

"You know darn well what one is, Mr. I Don't Combine Words. If I've told you once, I've told you a hundred times, but you choose not to listen. What's the point of sayin' you'll never go back to River Ranch if you ain't left it in the first place?"

"Do not throw veiled insults at me."

"Ha! There was nothing veiled about that."

Color flushed his cheeks. "Are you or are you not with

child?" In an unprecedented show of emotion, his hand gestured behind him at the shelf he'd fastened that held all our supplies. "You have not asked me for your monthlies."

"I...." Wait. "*What?*" Asked him? "What in the hell did you expect me to ask you?" If I could use one of my own damn tampons?

His eyebrows drew together. "You know exactly what I am referring to."

I crossed my arms, not sure I wanted to know where this conversation was going, because I could feel it coming. And that feeling was nothing good. In fact, it had fucked-up written all over it, and I'd bet my last can of fruit cocktail it had the markings of that sick cult he came from. "No, I most assuredly do not."

His penetrating gaze took me in and sized me up like he was looking for a lie. Then he spoke. "You have not asked me to put your monthlies in for you."

"Put... my...." No. "You mean...?" *No.* He couldn't. Absolutely not.

He said nothing.

"*Oh dear God in heaven,*" I whispered.

He remained silent.

I had to know. I didn't want to, but this... this level of seven ways from Sunday messed up, I couldn't let it go unchecked. Swallowing down disgust and a jealousy I wanted no part of, I asked. "Did the men on the compound.... Did you...?" I cleared my throat and rushed through the words. "Did y'all put tampons in women when they had their periods?"

He nodded once.

It was instant.

I slammed my hand over my mouth and shoved past him. I almost didn't make it out of the cabin before I threw up in the scrub brush surrounding the patch of dirt we'd cleared in front of the small porch.

But I didn't just throw up.

My stomach heaved, my body emptied everything it had, and my soul crushed in on itself.

My head was pounding, and I didn't want to cry anymore, but I couldn't stop it. Tears came, and they matched the vomit for intensity like it was a contest.

His hand appeared in front of me, holding a cup of water. "Drink."

Hearing his voice, knowing what we'd done earlier, how he'd taken me.... *Oh God*. This hurt, it hurt so bad, I didn't even want to think about it. He'd put tampons in other women. *Women*. Not woman. Not singular. Multiple. Hundreds for all I knew. Nothing, *nothing* about us together was new to him or special, and oh my fucking God, his question played in my head, over and over, hitting me like a sledgehammer.

Are you with child?

Are you with child?

Are you with child?

It repeated over and over like a cruel joke, and he knew to ask because he'd done this before. *He had children with other women.*

My stomach lurched, and I vomited again.

Chapter
TWENTY-SIX

Tarquin

SHE VOMITED A SECOND TIME.
She was with child.
I had seen it enough times on compound. Morning sickness, the females called it. Larger breasts, different moods, fuller hips before their stomachs swelled.

Despite the insults she threw at me, my cock grew hard at the thought of her body with my child. I held the water out again once the second wave of her nausea passed. "Drink this."

Without a word, without taking the water, she pushed past me and went back in the cabin.

I did not follow.

Fighting for patience, I stood a moment to collect myself, but she quickly came back out with her towel and our bar of soap. Aiming for our sun shower, she threw her towel over a tree branch and stripped her shirt off.

Deeply inhaling the morning air, I set the water down on the front step and walked over as she reached for the shower release. "Tilt your head back. I will help you." I had not yet refilled the reservoir from the well this morning. There would not be a lot of water.

"I don't need your help." She turned her back on me.

Ignoring her protest, I put my hand over hers on the release and grasped her hair. "Tilt." Not waiting for compliance, I pulled slightly on her hair and released the water.

Her mouth opened to protest, but she quickly shut it as I wet her hair.

"Give me the soap," I quietly demanded.

Defying me, she yanked out of my grasp. Working the bar into a lather, she hastily ran her hands over her long hair, but then her eyes met mine. With malice in her expression, she ran the bar between her legs. Vigorously.

Still in the jeans she had stolen from the addict for me, I stepped on the pallet with her and got in her face. "Do not provoke me." I knew what she was doing. Every morning after I took her, we bathed together. She knew how I felt about her washing my mark off.

The soap lathering into small white bubbles, she kept scrubbing.

"That will not undo what is done," I stated. "We need to have a discussion." She could not have a baby out here. I was not versed in childbirth, and neither was she.

"I'm not discussin' shit." Grabbing the water release, she turned her back on me and pulled it.

Water cascaded over both of us as she rinsed off.

Welcoming the coolness in the already humid day, I did not step back. The front of my jeans soaked, I waited until she had the soap off her body, then I put my head under what was left of the trickle of water.

Before she reached for it, I grabbed her towel. Wrapping it around her from behind, I used my arms to cocoon her.

Her muscles stiffened, and she fought my hold.

I held her tighter. "You are angry with me. I am angry with you. That does not change facts. You cannot have a baby out here. I do not have firsthand experience in childbirth, and the hurricane months are coming. We cannot stay here." After fifty-eight sunsets, we were also close to depleting the food supply she had stocked.

Her breathing faster than normal, she said nothing.

"It is time." My body was strong. I was ready. "We have discussed this." She had shown me on a map where the address was. We did not need to be out here anymore. No one had come looking for us after the initial fortnight, save wildlife and mosquitoes.

"*Experience in childbirth*," she mocked. "You sure about that?" She spun out of my grasp. "How many women have you knocked up?"

"Knocked up?" I did not know what I hated more, my sheltered upbringing or her manner of speech.

"Yeah, *knocked up*." She furiously rubbed the towel through her hair and over her supple flesh that was less soft than two months ago. "With child, impregnated, *expecting*." She spat the last word out with anger. "Do you even know how many little Tarquins are running around River Ranch?"

I gritted my teeth. "I told you I have not fathered any children before." Not that I knew of.

"Right." She snorted. "But you just *happen* to know when a woman's pregnant *and* how to put a damn tampon in for her." She threw the towel over the tree branch and yanked her sleeveless shirt back on.

"That is why you are angry?" Was she that irrational? "You are going to bring my past to present when your father hunted us for weeks?" Temper flaring, my tone matched. "Which one of us has a past that held us prisoner inside that cabin while men searched the woods around us for fourteen days? Because no one from compound came, tracking us like prey."

"It's *the* compound, THE!" she yelled. "Always *the compound*, not just compound! Learn how to speak!"

"I know exactly how to speak," I yelled back in my manner of speech before mimicking her accent. "You think I don't know how to fuckin' swear, drop *g*'s, and run my goddamn words together?"

She blinked.

I kept going with her manner of speech. "You think I ain't smart enough to mimic words and spit 'em back out?" I reverted to my accent. "I know exactly how you speak. But I am not ignorant enough to presume you will respect me for adapting to your ways. I am the man, you are the woman."

She blinked again.

The she pivoted and walked inside the cabin.

A moment later, she returned fully clothed with boots on and the canteen in her hand.

"Where are you going?" I demanded.

"Mama's. And don't try to stop me this time. It's been long enough. I'm goin' to check on her." Her voice dropped to a mutter. "Maybe she knows how to bring a child into this world, because I sure as hell don't."

"Wait." *Goddamn it.* The curse was silent, but no less indicative of how far I had come from River Ranch. "I will come with you." No matter our disagreement, no matter I did not approve of her seeing the hysterical woman who had had a hand in selling her off to the biker, I would not let her walk these woods alone. Besides, I was not too proud to consider that the hysterical woman she called Mother may have useful advice on childbirth. "Let me get dry clothes."

She did not acknowledge me, but neither did she walk away.

Stepping inside the cabin, I hung my wet jeans on a wooden hook I had fastened to the wall, and I retrieved my only article of clothing from River Ranch. Donning the jeans I had been stabbed in that now had a mended leg courtesy of my woman, I felt a pang of remorse for my heated words to her earlier. I did not hate kissing her. I hated that I was not skilled at it.

Pulling on a T-shirt and dry socks, I shook out my wet hair that was too long before stepping back into my boots. Grabbing one of the guns, I tucked it in my back waistband. Then I took one of the few plastic bottles of water we had left and I exited the cabin. Retrieving the padlock from the inside, I moved it to the outside and locked the door.

When I turned, she was staring at me, but she did not speak.

"Let us go."

With merely a nod, she turned toward the narrow trail and began walking.

We traveled in silence for several kilometers. When we made it out of the thickest part of the woods and got closer to her father's land, she abruptly stopped and turned to face me.

"Maybe you're right." Her gaze briefly met mine before she looked away. "Maybe it's time you go talk to that recruiter."

I stilled.

She had yet to agree with me that it was time. Her excuses were numerous, invalid, and based on fear—she wasn't ready to leave, her father could still be looking for us, River Stephens could be looking for me, she had to check on her mother, my stab wounds still looked unhealed. I had not started to challenge her excuses until recently when our food supply was getting low.

Waiting to see if she had more to say on the subject, I did not respond.

"I don't know what all it'll entail gettin' you into the Army, and like we discussed before, I don't know what all they'll want from you, official-wise, like paperwork or whatever or how we even get that kinda stuff." She looked back at me. "But maybe it's time you go and find out."

When I continued to say nothing, she kept talking.

"You've been runnin' in the woods every day, choppin' wood, doin' pull-ups on the tree by the shower…." She looked at her feet as she toed the damp earth underfoot. "You're strong enough now, Tarquin."

I did not disagree. I was. But suddenly, now that she was telling me to go, hesitation pushed at my conscience. "Will your mother alert your father when you call on her?"

She shrugged. "Not if I take her phone away first."

"What if he is already there?"

"He won't be. Last few years he's always come at night, and besides, if he is, we'll see his SUV."

Then there was no more decision to make. "You will stay with her until I return for you."

She let out a half snort, half sound of indignation. "It's practically a twenty-mile hike one way to that Army recruiter's. I don't know if I can take Mama for that long."

"You used to live with her."

"Yeah, but that was before." She looked up at me, and her voice softened. "Before I got used to bein' with you."

"Shaila—"

She held a hand up. "I get it. I won't get you all the time, not when you join the Army and go off fightin' or wherever they send you. I know they'll get first rights to you. I get that's what enlistin' is all about."

I did not comment.

"So let's just stick to our plan, okay?"

"All right." I nodded.

"Great," she said without enthusiasm. "Let's get on with it. You can walk me to Mama's, and I'll hold out there as long as I can. Which, for the record, she may be my mama, but I was never her biggest fan. Me and her? We don't got a whole lot in common."

"You will be fine with her for one day."

My woman almost smiled. "You said day and not sunup or sundown. But let's not get ahead of ourselves. I'm comin' home to the cabin tonight."

"I do not want you walking these woods alone."

She scoffed. "I walked them all by myself for years before I met you. Even at night. It's how I found you, ain't it?"

Her voice took on a tone. "Who knows? Maybe I'll find another River Ranch castoff."

My jaw clenched at the thought, even though I knew it was a highly unlikely impossibility. "I will come for you at your mother's."

She raised an eyebrow in challenge. "You can try. I may or may not be there still." She turned back toward the deer trail we'd been walking on through the swamp. "And for the record? I ain't mad at you for, you know, the sex." Her voice quieted, and she looked over her shoulder at me. "It felt good, even if you didn't wanna kiss my mouth."

Regret formed in my throat. "I wanted to kiss you."

She stopped walking and turned. "Then why did you say you didn't like kissin'?"

I stared at her grass-green eyes. I did not regret how I took her earlier, but maybe I regretted my words. "You were not satisfied with me. You wanted more."

Her face fell. "I'm always satisfied with you. I just wanted you to kiss me."

"You wanted more," I corrected.

"If you wanna call kissin' more, then yeah, I guess I did want more."

"I gave you a release." What more did she want?

She exhaled as if for patience. "I know. You always take care of me like that, and trust me, I appreciate it." Her cheeks reddened, and she averted her gaze. "That's one of the things I love about you."

My heart beat faster, and my pulse quickened. I did not say anything. I did not move.

She stepped forward and placed her hand on my chest.

She looked up at me, and sunlight hit her face. It highlighted her smooth skin and flushed cheeks, and it made the red strands in her hair more pronounced. I did not know a prettier woman.

Her voice quieted. "You know what I'm gonna say, don't you?"

My cock stiffened, and my hands fisted. "No." Possibly.

"I love you, Tarquin Scott."

I swallowed.

"I love you like a sunrise, and I just wanted you to kiss me so I could feel your love for me, because I know I may never get those words from you."

I grabbed her chin and jaw in one hand. Then I gave her words I did know the meaning of. "I am inside you."

Having nothing greater to give her than that, I kissed her.

Chapter
TWENTY-SEVEN

Shaila

He kissed me passionately, and I melted. But then he pulled back, and it was over much too quickly.

My face flushed, my skin heated, desire pulsed painfully between my legs. Despite every hard inch of him being inside me so many times today already, I wanted more.

I always wanted more of him.

He was my addiction.

I didn't know if that was normal, or even healthy, but I didn't care.

Tarquin Scott was my world, and I wanted to keep him forever.

That's why I'd been trying to put him off going to that recruiter's, but even I couldn't deny we were short on time now. I hadn't gotten my period in two cycles, and it didn't take a genius to figure out I was pregnant.

With his baby.

My heart melted at the very thought the same time fear snuck around the joy and gave me anxiety. I wasn't stupid.

I knew I couldn't safely have a baby out here, and we were getting low on food.

So the recruiter.

It was time.

Wary, turned on, thankful for his kiss, I put my hand in his and squeezed. "Thank you."

With blue eyes so clear they were almost haunting, and muscles that seemed twice as big as when I first saw him, he stared down at me. "For what?"

"Kissin' me."

He looked away. "I am not skilled at kissing." His voice dropped. "That is why I said what I said."

Confusion turned to understanding. "You said you didn't like kissin' me because you think you're bad at it?"

He didn't look at me. "Yes."

"Please look at me."

Slow, deliberate, he turned his head, and a storm of unease rioted in his eyes.

I cupped his jaw as scratchy two-day growth tickled my fingers. "You're the best kisser I know, and I love every second of every one of your kisses."

He inhaled as a slight frown formed, but the storm in his eyes, it quieted. "It is time to go." He grasped my wrist and gently removed my hand from his face, but then he didn't let go of my hand.

Truth be told, I didn't want to go just yet. I wanted to stand a bit longer and simply hold his hand. Because just as I was holding his, he was holding mine, and that wasn't something he did often. Small acts of affection were not in his repertoire because Tarquin Scott didn't touch unnecessarily. So when I got a gesture of affection like this, I wanted to hold on to it. Literally.

But he had a long walk ahead of him, and the path through the scrub brush, if you could call it that, wasn't more than a single foot wide and we couldn't walk the rest of the way to Mama's hand in hand.

"Right. Time to go." Reluctantly, I let go of his hand and stepped forward. "But remember everythin' we talked about when you get to the recruiters."

"I will remember." His voice was not loud, but it carried from behind me at the same time as it sounded like it was a part of the Glades, like he belonged here as much as the slash pines and mangroves.

A pace ahead of him, I wasn't laying eyes on him, but awareness crawled up my spine the same as it did every time he was near. I was so attuned to him now, my body knew when he was close. I had to shove down the urge to turn around and launch myself into his arms. Not to mention I was fighting off a horrible feeling of dread that made me want to turn us around and head us right back to our cabin.

Forcing myself to stay focused on the conversation, I pushed the unease away and reminded him of what we'd talked about last week. "Don't forget to take everythin' they say with a grain of salt. I don't want you signin' anythin' you ain't one-hundred percent sure of. Even if they offer you money or some kinda sign-up bonus. Don't give them your John Hancock just because they make it sound like they're doin' you a favor."

"John Hancock?"

"Yeah, your signature. Like when you write your

name, but in cursive, not print, so it's, you know, fancy and official."

"I do not have a signature."

"Everybody's got a signature."

"I do not." He was quiet a moment, then, "I do not know how to write."

Shock stopped me in my tracks, and I turned to face him. "Really?"

"I am illiterate," he said without shame or intonation or any emotion whatsoever. "I do not know how to read or write."

"But the map. We looked at it together. You said you memorized the way to the address." How could he not know how to read or write?

"I did memorize it."

"But you can't read?"

He shook his head once. "Or write. There was no use for it in my assigned duty on the compound."

I was so busy picking my jaw up off the ground, I didn't even notice he said *the* compound. "But you're smart. And you talk fancy." And he was the most observant person I knew.

"Just because I do not know how to read does not mean I do not know how to speak properly. Slang was not allowed on the compound."

"No, no, I get it. I'm just… surprised is all." And the whole situation made my heart break for him and the childhood he'd had. "All those nights I read to you and you never read to me, I just thought it was because you liked hearin' my voice."

"I do."

I fought a smile and lost. "Good to know. Well, okay then. How about you bring back any paperwork they give you at the recruiter's office, and I can read it to you. We'll go over it together." I raised an eyebrow. "And then I can teach you how to read. And write." Lord help us both. "Sound good?"

He fingered a strand of my hair. "I will not want to read or write when I return."

I blushed hard as every nerve ending in my body pulsed with desire. "Okay, in the morning then."

"Not then either."

A nervous laugh bubbled up, and I stood on tiptoe. "Okay then, Mr. Scott, how about you tell me when you're ready and we'll go from there?" I kissed his cheek.

As his gaze pierced mine, he gripped the side of my face, and then he did what he always did when he was done talking about something. He abruptly changed the subject. "I do not think it is wise if your mother sees me, but I will escort you inside if you prefer."

My body melting under his dominant touch, I struggled to switch gears. "No, you're right. I was gonna suggest the same. In fact, I was gonna tell Mama I didn't know where you were. There's no sense in giving her or Daddy a reason to start searchin' again."

"Do not tell her where we are staying."

"Not a chance. I know anythin' I say to her, she'll tell Daddy the second I'm out the door. Don't worry, I got this." I knew how to handle Mama.

"I am not denying you the chance to see her, but it is not without risk."

"I know." We had talked about it plenty over the past few weeks, and he'd never outright told me no. He'd just said it wasn't a good idea, and I understood that. "But if you're joinin' the Army and I'm comin' with you, then this may be my last chance to see her for a long while." If ever. I wasn't under any delusion that Mama hadn't sold me out just the same as Daddy by being complicit, but she was still my mama, and I wanted to see her one last time.

My man nodded once, then he took me completely off guard.

Wrapping his strong, muscular arms around me, he pulled me close and for a long moment, he simply hugged me.

Then he pulled back and kissed my forehead. "I will walk you to the clearing and wait for you to get inside. If everything is fine, move the curtains on the front window. Then I will go to the recruiter's and return for you as soon as I can."

Not ready to say goodbye yet, unsure about how I felt being away from him, I put my arms around him one more time. "Okay. But make sure you come back for me." And I almost didn't say anything, but I couldn't not bring it up. "And if you see any Lone Coaster bikers, or bikers at all for that matter, you hide." I pulled back to look up at him. "You hear me? You hide."

He cupped my cheek. "I am armed. Do not worry."

"Come back for me, Tarquin Scott." I didn't know if I was warning him that he'd better, or begging him to keep his promise, but no matter, I had to say the words.

As rare as a cold sunrise in the Glades, the corner of his mouth almost tipped up and Tarquin Scott gave me his version of a smile. "Always."

Chapter
TWENTY-EIGHT

Tarquin

I waited until she appeared in the front window. She grasped the curtain and moved it back and forth. She could not see me where I was standing hidden in the shadows, but I nodded anyway.

Then I walked.

The further I went, the more the landscape changed. Woods gave way to fields, which gave way to lawns and houses, then buildings and busy roads. Everything I had been warned about growing up, I saw. River Stephens had referred to it as urban sprawl and the work of the devil. The scent of exhaust fumes, the rush of cars driving fast and honking, the scent of stale food from buildings with garish signs, I did not disagree.

Staying alert, I walked until I found the address.

The Army recruiter's office.

Four walls, concrete block, freshly painted, and the same symbol tattooed on the brother's arm from River Ranch was on the glass front door.

For a long moment, I stared. I did not know why that brother all those years ago had made me memorize this address. I did not know what he saw in me that compelled him to reach out to me like he did. But as I stood in front of a building that was nicer than any on River Ranch, I felt the depth of an isolated upbringing manipulated by a madman.

Hating River Stephens even more, I took one last breath of smog-tainted humidity and pushed open the glass door.

"Welcome!" A man who had a decade more turns around the sun than I was sitting behind a desk. Wearing a uniform and a smile, he stood. "I'm Staff Sergeant Miller. How can I help you?"

The air-conditioned room smelled crisp and fresh. Carpeted flooring underfoot muffled my steps. Walls of fine plaster surrounded furniture that was not roughhewn by hand. I had never stepped foot in such a fine place. "I want to be an Army Ranger."

His smile wide and genuine, his uniform fitted to his body, his hair cut even and shorn close to his head—his appearance made me acutely aware of my too long hair, worn clothes, and my face that had not seen a razor since sunset before last.

"Well, you've come to the right place, and that's a high ambition. I like it. A man's got to know what he wants, right?" He gestured toward the chair in front of his desk without waiting for a response. "Have a seat."

I sat. In a chair not hand-carved from slash pine.

The man's smile held as he took his seat again. "What's your name?"

"Tarquin Scott."

He nodded as if I had told him something he already knew. "That's not a first name you usually hear. Is it a family name?"

I did not want to engage in conversation. I wanted to join the Army and get back to my woman. "No." No one on compound had the same namesake as me.

"Well, I like it." His hands moved across a keyboard as he looked at a screen facing him. "Let's get some basic information on you, and then I can walk you through the process and answer any questions you might have." He glanced up at me. "Sound good?"

"Yes." Uneasiness, more so than on the journey here, settled in. I had only seen a computer once before in River Stephens's quarters, and it had made me uncomfortable then like this one was making me now.

"Okay." The recruiter smiled again then looked at his screen as his fingers moved on the keyboard. "Is your name spelled T-A-R-Q-U-I-N with one N?"

I did not know. "Yes."

"Perfect. And Scott is with two Ts?"

Uncomfortable, not knowing the answer to that question either, I shifted in my chair. "Yes."

"Birth date?"

"What?"

"Age?"

Fifteen turns around the sun, eighteen, twenty, maybe more—I did not know my exact age. I only knew the turns since I had been counting them myself. Remembering my woman's reaction when she had asked me the same question and I had given her the honest answer, I did not tell the recruiter fifteen turns. I picked a different number. "Twenty."

"Date you were born?"

I made one up. "November first."

"Year?"

I had already told him. "Twenty years ago."

He glanced up at me, and his gaze ran over my shoulders and arms before he looked back at his screen. "Right. Twenty." His fingers moved across the keys. "Address?"

I did not know how he got his hair cut so even. "I do not have one." I would ask my woman to shear my hair tonight. My knife was sharp enough.

The recruiter's voice quieted. "No shame in being homeless. If you're currently in a shelter, we can use that address."

"I am not homeless." The cabin was shelter. "I come from the Glades."

He nodded again, but a line formed between his eyes. "Okay. Well, I just need an address of where you live, so I can enter it into the database."

"Where I live has no address." And no running water and no electricity and no fine furnishings like this space.

The Staff Sergeant let out a humorless laugh. "Pretty sure everywhere in America has an address these days. If you can't find it on Google Maps, it doesn't exist."

I did not know what Google Maps was. I did not comment.

The recruiter's eyebrows drew together in suspicion. "Do you have a record?"

I was not ignorant to the term. There were brothers on compound who had served time in jail. "No."

"Where in the Everglades did you say you're from?"

"I did not specify."

"Right." He nodded slowly. "So…?"

Not offering any more information, not moving, I held his stare and remained still.

His frown dissipated as he studied me. Then a small smile spread his thin lips. "I think you might actually make one hell of a Ranger, son."

"That is my intent."

His expression turned serious again. "I can see that. But tell me something…." His gaze dropped from mine as he looked at his lap before looking back up at me. "Do you think the United States Army will spend the money required to train you to become a soldier if they don't know the simplest of things about you, like where you come from?"

"I do not presume to know what the Army thinks."

The recruiter exhaled sharply. "That attitude won't help you, son."

Hiding my frustration, I answered evenly. "I have no attitude. I was giving an honest answer to your inquiry. I want to be a Ranger. That is all."

Pushing back in his chair, the man clasped his hands. Then his expression softened for the first time since I'd walked through the door. "Okay, son, I'm going to offer you a deal. How about for the next…" He glanced at a clock on the wall. "…five minutes, you have my complete attention and discretion. Anything you want to tell me will be between just us. No judgment," he added.

Weighing the possibility of his honesty, I remained still.

My woman had said people would want to use me.

I did not doubt her.

I knew the rarity of my situation. No one left River Ranch of their own accord.

What I did not know was how the recruiter would react to the truth. Which left me two choices.

One a risk, the other cowardly.

Walking out would mean failure of the one promise I had made to myself when the first blow struck my body after River Stephens condemned me to death. Walking out of the Army recruiter's would be the cowardly move. I knew that.

But try as I might, time had put distance between me and the many sunsets ago I had made that promise, and I no longer harbored the singular taste for revenge in my mouth. I now tasted my woman.

Soft thighs, sweet cunt, full breasts—those were the tastes on my tongue now. The flavors I woke to every sunrise and bedded down to every night. With my cock swollen inside her tight cunt, there was no room for revenge. I had my woman to take care of now.

Which left the other choice.

Confide in the recruiter.

Lay down honesty in offering and stand tall to its repercussions.

My woman with child, there was no choice.

Briefly taking in the round object on the wall with two hands that ticked, I looked the recruiter dead in the eye. "We did not have clocks at River Ranch."

The recruiter inhaled sharply, and the air inside the room that was free of dirt and dust and the scent of unwashed bodies turned thick with tension.

The clock ticked.

My heart pumped.

The air conditioning blew cool air over my flesh.

I did not move. I did not offer more. I did not elaborate. I waited.

Eyes wide, expression frozen in shock, the recruiter remained silent. Then he nodded, slowly. "No, I would imagine you didn't have many clocks on River Ranch."

Nothing in his tone to indicate I was in danger, I gave him the rest of the truth. "I do not know my exact age. I do not have an address. I do not have a number associated with my birth or a record thereof to my knowledge. I did not have a last name that differed from the madman who resides over River Ranch until I gave myself one."

I debated continuing.

The recruiter waited.

Practicality prevailed. I had more to lose withholding information. "My wife is with child. We cannot live off the land while she prepares for birth. I am not versed in childbirth. I would like to become a Ranger. My aim is true. My body is strong. My mind is sharp."

"I don't doubt any of that, son. Can I ask you a question?"

"Yes."

"Is your wife from River Ranch?"

"No, she is not."

He looked surprised. "May I ask if you are legally married?"

I hesitated.

He explained. "The reason I ask is because the Army is

not going to provide any married benefits if you aren't legally married."

"She is mine. I fought for rights for her."

The man rubbed a hand over his chin. "Okay, son. I'm not going to lie. This is all way above my pay grade. But as a father, I am concerned for both of you. You say you are living off the land?"

"As I have always done." Defensiveness colored my tone. "I know how to take care of her."

"I know you do, son. I don't doubt for one second you know way more than me in that regard, and I'm fourth generation Floridian. My great-grandma raised her boys on swamp cabbage and deer meat. I know it can be done." He looked at me for a long moment. "But I need to be truthful with you now. You ready for this?"

My muscles stiffened. "Yes."

"I can't enlist you. The Army requires proper identification, and you have none. It would take you months to go through proper channels to get a birth certificate, assuming you could get someone with proper identification to verify it for you, which, since you're sitting here, I'm going to assume that isn't possible because I've heard no one makes it out of River Ranch alive. That said, that very fact may be your ticket into the Army. But you would have to be willing to have a conversation with a friend of mine at the FBI and tell him everything you just told me."

"No." I stood. "No FBI." The last time we encountered them on compound, they shot females and children.

Holding his hands out in a placating gesture, the recruiter stood as well. "I know the FBI is probably a threatening concept to you. I'm assuming you lived through their last raid of River Ranch?"

Short and clipped, I nodded once.

"My friend wasn't part of that, I swear. He's a good man, and he definitely won't want any harm to come to you or your wife. All he'll want is information. In exchange, you can ask him to expedite paperwork for you. Get you the proper documentation you need for identification." His gaze held mine. "Then you can join the Army." His voice quieted with conviction. "You could become a Ranger."

Fuck.

Fuck.

"If I give information to the FBI, River Stephens will know I am alive." And then I would be hunted.

The man's face paled. "He thinks you're dead?"

"I was vanquished."

"Pardon?"

I gave him the whole truth. "I was beaten, stabbed and thrown out of River Ranch. Unconscious, assuming I was dead, they carried my body off compound and left me in the swamp for the elements."

The man looked horror-struck. "How on earth did you survive?"

I gave the simplest of answers. "I wanted to be a Ranger."

He stared at me. "Is that why you were kicked out?"

"No. I gave a female a flower. It was against the rules."

"Jesus Christ," he whispered.

I made the decision. "Call your friend. I will speak with him."

Chapter
TWENTY-NINE

Shaila

"No, Mama." Out of patience, I yelled, "I ain't stayin' and you ain't getting' your cell phone back to call Daddy." Lord have mercy, how had I put up with this woman?

"But, Shaila," she whined, "we need Daddy. He'll fix this. He'll fix everything." She swayed on her feet.

I'd had it.

I didn't even know why I'd wanted to come back here.

The carpet was old and nasty. The house smelled like her weed. There was a month's worth of dishes in the kitchen, and cockroaches were feasting on every single crumb they could find on the dirty countertops.

I couldn't stay here another second.

"I'm done, Mama. There's nothin' to fix. I ain't Daddy's or anyone else's property to be sold or bartered or used as some kinda pawn, so get that through your head. I ain't becomin' some biker's old lady and that's final. It was real… interestin' seein' you, but now I'm goin', and I ain't ever comin' back.

Have a nice life." Or don't. I no longer cared. "I'll leave your cell phone in the garage on the counter. Guess you'll be able to call Daddy as soon as you muster the courage to walk out there."

"Shaila!" she cried in her pathetic voice. "Don't do this! *Don't go.*"

I turned toward the door and yanked it open.

Before I could make it outside to the fresh air not tainted with her drug abuse, she grabbed my arm.

"Mama," I warned. "Let go."

With surprising strength for someone as skinny as she was, her fingers dug into my arm. "No! You ain't leaving till your Daddy gets here."

"If you know what's best for you, Mama, you'll let go before I force you to let go." No longer worried about making waves with her, she had no pull over me.

Her face contorted with a sick look I'd never seen, and anger laced her voice. "You're *not* leavin'." She reached for me with her other hand.

It was instinctual.

I drew back and slapped her.

Rage and the imprint of my hand reddened her face, and her hands came up.

Too late, I realized her intent.

The force of her open palms smacked against my chest and she shoved me with all of her might.

No purchase, not expecting her to fight back, I flew backward out the front door, tripped on the broken top step, and I fell off the porch.

My back hit the hard ground, air left my lungs and sharp pain shot through my midsection.

I opened my mouth to scream, but it wasn't my voice that broke the humid Florida afternoon.

"*Shaila!*" Mama cried out.

Everything went black.

Chapter
THIRTY

Tarquin

A MAN IN FORMAL DRESS WALKED INTO THE OFFICE WITH purpose. Glancing at me, he set a leather bag on the desk and nodded at the recruiter. "Staff Sergeant." He looked back at me. "You must be Tarquin Scott."

I did not offer my hand, and neither did he. "Yes."

"I'm Special Agent Tom Morrison with the FBI." The man tipped his chin at the seat next to me. "May I?"

It was not my domain to command, but I answered anyway. "Yes."

Before taking the seat, he glanced at the recruiter. "Thanks for the call, Miller. Lock the door so we're not interrupted."

The recruiter stood without comment and did as the agent said.

The agent opened his leather case, pulled out a small black device with buttons, a flat device with a screen, and a cell phone. He placed them all on the desk, then he sat. Meeting my gaze, his brown eyes expressed intellect and gravity. "I'm going to cut right to the chase. You're from River Ranch."

I nodded as the recruiter sat back down.

"Staff Sergeant told me you want to join the Army, but you don't have any identification or background."

"I was here when he made the call. I am aware of what he told you."

The agent nodded. "Good. Then you understand the rarity of this situation. I've never met a living witness from River Ranch."

"No one leaves River Ranch." Not alive. I could attest to that fact.

"I understand that. What I don't understand is how you got out."

"I was vanquished."

Without comment, the agent waited for more information.

I studied his face. No formal education, I did not have the advantage here. But I had seen many different sides of what man was capable of. Expression gave away intent. Malice could not be hidden. Evil had a silver tongue, and trust was merely a word. These things I knew.

It was why I would not give specifics away freely. "If you would like information on River Ranch, I will need assurances."

"Which are?"

"Admittance into the United States Army and Ranger training and living quarters for me and my wife, as well as medical assistance."

The agent frowned. "You're married?"

"Yes."

"Not legally," the recruiter interjected. "I would need the proper documentation to accommodate her."

The agent glanced at the recruiter, nodded and looked back at me. "Is your wife injured?"

"She is with child."

"You get healthcare in the Army, your medical will be covered for both of you." The agent stared at me a moment. "Is she from River Ranch?"

"No."

The agent blinked but hid his surprise well. "I can't speak for the Army and what accommodations they're willing to make for an enlisted married man, but I am willing to work with you if the Staff Sergeant is."

The recruiter opened his mouth.

The agent held up his hand to him. "That said, placement into the Ranger program is not something anyone can give you. You have to earn it with discipline, determination and strength."

"I will earn it." I had no doubt.

The agent did not question my statement but merely nodded. "All right, then in exchange for information on River Ranch that I can use to dismantle River Stephens's weapons cache, I'm willing to get you the proper background and paperwork needed to enlist and I'll help facilitate a marriage license. In addition, the FBI currently has a reward for information that could lead to River Stephens's arrest. If the information you give me is solid, you will qualify for that monetary reward."

Saying nothing, I catalogued his body language.

Not fidgeting, not shifting in his seat, gaze steady, he did not show any signs of dishonesty as he spoke again. "If it makes you more comfortable, after you tell me what you know, I'll throw witness protection on the table. If needed, I'll get the US Marshal Service involved and get you and your wife a new identity."

I did not need a new identity when I did not have one to begin with, but I was not ignorant. My woman was identifiable. "I will reserve the right to discuss that with my wife."

"As you should." The agent reached into this bag and pulled out some papers. Setting them on the desk between us, he put his hand on top of them. "These forms are what you will need. If we have a deal, I will sign off on them and walk them through processing myself, then you will have what you need for Staff Sergeant Miller."

"How long?" I did not know what processing entailed, but it sounded as if it were not immediate.

"For the paperwork?" the agent asked.

"Yes." Glancing at the clock, I fought off another wave of uneasiness at my woman being alone with her mother. I did not know how to use the device on the wall to tell time, and I did not know how long I had been here, but I could see the sun starting its afternoon descent.

"A week, two. Max."

I stood. "No, thank you." We would be out of proper food within a week, and my woman was already too thin for being with child.

"Wait." The agent stood. "Negotiate."

"I am not here to negotiate." The lie rolling easily off

my tongue, I compounded it. "You want what I know, but I do not need what you are offering."

The agent held my gaze. "Then why are you here?"

Taken unawares by the question, I did not answer it. "I spoke my piece. My requirements have not changed."

"I've met your requirements," he countered.

Unused to argument except from my woman, I chose my words carefully. "Whatever information you are seeking to attain about River Ranch, I have. My worth to you is greater than your offer of one to two weeks."

The agent nodded slowly. "I'll expedite the paperwork then."

I waited.

His hands went to his hips. "One to two days for your paperwork. The marriage license may take more. Your wife will need to provide her own identification."

"She does not have any." Not that I had seen.

The agent frowned again. "And she isn't River Ranch?"

"No."

"Is she illegal?"

"I do not know what means," I admitted.

"Was she born in the United States," the agent clarified.

"Yes. Florida."

The agent inhaled. "Okay, if she isn't River Ranch, she should have identification. A driver's license, a birth certificate, passport, something."

There was nothing like that in the cabin. "She has none of that."

"What's her name?"

I hesitated.

The agent eyed me. "So far, up to this point, everything we have discussed is between you, me, and Staff Sergeant Miller. Unless she is already in witness protection, there's nothing you're risking by telling me her name."

I did not believe him. There was always risk. Putting her name in the same breath with mine was a risk to her.

"We're still speaking confidentially," the agent persuaded.

I did not see a way around this if I wanted to get her into living quarters provided by the Army. "Shaila Hawkins."

The two men looked at one another.

The agent spoke first. "All right, I'm hoping this is one hell of a coincidence, but I have to ask. Is she related to Stone Hawkins?"

I said nothing.

"Jesus Christ." The agent sat down before glancing at the recruiter. "Did you know about this?"

Eyes wide, the recruiter shook his head.

The shock on his face now hidden, the agent looked back at me. "How is she related to Stone?"

"She is his daughter," I admitted.

"Does he know you're with her?" the agent asked.

Defiant, I replied, "I fought for rights to her." She was mine.

The recruiter mouthed the word *wow*.

Keeping his expression guarded, the agent merely nodded. "So Stone has seen you? He knows where you're from?"

"We have not met in person."

"But does he know what you look like?" the agent persisted.

"I do not know." The hysterical female could have given him a description.

"You sure?" The agent's eyes narrowed. "Because there's quite a rumor floating around about a mass shooting out at his place on the edge of the Glades that happened a couple months back."

"I do not know anything about any rumors." I only knew the truth.

The agent stood again and paced. "Of course, we have no bodies and no proof." He turned and looked pointedly at me. "But if we had more information about it…." He trailed off.

I said nothing.

"We've had Stone Hawkins on our radar for years. Gun running, drugs, prostitution." He paused for effect. "Murder."

"I have not met him." I only had him in my sights.

"But you're married to his daughter?"

I remained silent.

The agent held my gaze for a long moment. Then he shook his head. "*Christ.* No wonder you want into the military." He pulled a pad of paper out of his leather bag and some photographs. "Okay, are we going to do this? Do we have a deal?"

"Will my wife be granted living quarters?"

The agent looked at the recruiter. "That's up to the Staff Sergeant. Miller?"

The recruiter cleared his throat. "If you are legally married, the Army requires you to provide adequate support for your dependents, including housing. Because of this, you will receive a housing allowance at the 'with dependent' rate.

However, while you complete basic training, you will live in the barracks and your wife will need other accommodations. There is on-base family housing or, if you choose, she can be off-base and you can use your monthly housing allowance. Once you complete basic training and receive your assignment, the housing choices for her may change, but she will always have housing as long as she is your dependent."

"Jesus Christ, Miller," the agent snapped. "Do what you have to do and just get him into married housing."

The recruiter nodded once. "Okay. I'll make it happen."

The agent looked back at me. "Good?"

I did not pretend to understand how the inner workings of the Army operated, but I understood enough to know she would be safe in quarters with proper plumbing and electricity. That only left one issue. Her safety from her father while I was unable to be with her.

But in order to secure that, I would need to tell the agent the full truth of the situation, which I did not want to do in front of the recruiter, even though the agent had already mentioned the incident on her father's land.

Having already come this far, I cleared my throat. "I have one last issue that I need to discuss with you alone."

Chapter
THIRTY-ONE

Shaila

"Shaila, Shaila." My shoulders shook, and unbearable pain shot through my middle.

"Shaila, wake up!"

My face was slapped.

I sucked in a breath that felt like icicles stabbing me and forced an eye open.

"Oh thank God, you scared the living daylights outta me."

I blinked, but I couldn't focus. "Mama?"

Her shaking hand brushed my hair back as her tears dripped on my face. "I'm sorry, baby. I didn't mean to push you. Forgive me. Just get up and we'll go inside. It'll be okay." She jostled my shoulders again. "Come on, just get up now."

"Don't," I protested, testing a shallow breath. "Don't shake me." Oh sweet Jesus, I hurt.

"Sorry, sorry." Mama leaned back as her hands ran down my arms. "Just get up now. You gotta get up."

A sudden fever flushed my face, and everything spun for a moment before I tried another breath.

"Come on, Shaila. You gotta get up. You gotta get my phone from the garage so we can call Daddy. He'll know what to do."

"Do?" I tried to push up, but searing pain cramped my whole stomach and made my vision swim.

"Yes, yes," she rushed through the words. "We need him, baby. You need him. He can fix this." Her voice broke and more tears fell down her face. "He can fix you."

Oh dear God in heaven. "Mama, I told you, I'm not callin' Daddy." The words like sandpaper in my throat, it hurt to even talk. "I ain't never callin' him again."

"But you're bleedin'." Mama choked on a sob. "You're bleedin' bad."

"What?" My head spun. "Where?"

Mama's gaze cut to my legs.

Taking another shallow breath, cursing every pain in my middle, I got one elbow under me. "I ain't bleedin', Mama. I'm fi—"

Oh.

Dear.

God.

Blood.

EVERYWHERE.

Between my legs.

I couldn't get air in for a sob or a scream. My mouth opened, but nothing came out.

My baby.

My baby.

A choked cry ripped from my lungs as pain cut me deep. "My baby!"

Chapter
THIRTY-TWO

Tarquin

The recruiter stepped outside, and I told the agent everything he needed to know about River Ranch and River Stephens, including where I had buried the bodies that met untimely deaths. Then I told him about the events that led to me and my woman hiding in the Glades. "That is why my wife will need protection from her father."

The agent did not respond. He blinked.

"She needs protection," I repeated.

"No, I heard you. I get it." The agent slowly shook his head. "I just… goddamn, I was not expecting all of this."

I did not care what he expected and he did not get it. "Her father will use her as leverage to get to me." It was what River Stephens would do. "If I am not with her, she is vulnerable."

Looking past me, the agent frowned. "How many of Stone's LCs did you say you shot?"

I was not repeating myself. I had already told him everything, and my patience was wearing thin. Dusk was passing and I was out of time. I needed to get to her. "I gave you the information you need on River Ranch." I gave him all the leverage I had. "How will you protect my wife?"

"Okay." He nodded as if clearing his head. Then he sat up straight and focused his gaze on me. "All right. This is what we're going to do. We'll get the Marshals Service involved and we'll WITSEC her. She'll get a new identity, background, the works." Searching my face, he paused. "You'll need the same, and you'll both be relocated. The Lone Coasters Motorcycle Club has hundreds of members up and down Florida's east coast. We can't hide her in state, no more than we could protect you from Stone Hawkins issuing a hit on you if he finds out you're alive."

I did not care about myself. "Protect her. I will be fine. I do not need a new identity."

The agent exhaled. "Okay, look. Any woman attached to the name Tarquin Scott is going to be a target from here on out because Stone Hawkins now knows your name. You have to understand that. And even though no bodies were discovered at Hawkins's place, and no one's come forward about a dozen dead bikers—which, trust me, we usually hear about—you're still a target. You need to play this safe for her and for you."

I did not correct his inaccurate death count. I was weighing his statement. I wanted to protect my woman, but I did not want to hide. Not hiding gave me opportunity if River did send someone from the compound after me.

The agent continued. "You also need to realize if what you say is true, and I don't doubt that it is because who would make something like that up? You're going to have a bigger problem than just keeping your wife safe if Stone Hawkins comes forward with any of this. I'm not putting any of what you told me about Hawkins in my report. I'm sticking to the River Ranch script and getting you into the Army after we secure new WITSEC identities for you. But that doesn't mean he won't come forward with his own evidence against you in order to get you put away."

"I will handle it if he does." My aim was true and patience afforded opportunity. I stood. "I will be here tomorrow morning as instructed. Have the paperwork ready."

The agent stood slowly as if he had aged since walking into the recruiter's office. "I'll have everything I promised. The US Marshal Service will be here in the morning with me as well as my superior so he can sign off on some of the paperwork, so make sure you bring your wife."

I nodded once and turned toward the door.

"Hey," the agent called. "You need a ride?"

"No vehicle can go where I am going."

The agent nodded as he studied me. Then he surprised me. "We'll stop Stephens."

No, he would not. "Do not underestimate his cunning."

"You already gave me his hiding places. He won't have anywhere to go next time we raid the compound. We'll catch him and we'll stop him from brainwashing any more of those people."

He would not catch him or stop him. There was only one way to stop a madman like River Stephens, and it was the same way to stop a man like Stone Hawkins—you had to take their lives away from them. "You will not stop him."

But I would.

I would stop both of them.

Chapter
THIRTY-THREE

Tarquin

I WALKED OUT OF THE RECRUITER'S OFFICE.

Standing in the fading dusk, the recruiter looked at me with concern. "All done?"

"Yes. I will be back tomorrow with my wife. The agent says he will be here with the paperwork."

"If he says he'll be here, he'll be here." The recruiter handed me a bag he was holding. "Here. I figured you must be hungry. I got you a couple sandwiches and two bottles of water from the deli across the street. Nothing fancy, but they're good."

"Thank you." Taking the bag, I scanned the view in front of me in the fading light. Neither dusk nor nightfall could disguise the endless amount of asphalt, garish lit-up signs or lack of unspoiled earth.

I did not want to live in this world where paved roads and buildings as far as the eye could see stamped out nature. The yearning for my woman and the solace of forest around me with the sound of the wind through the trees was so great, I felt sick. But this was the world I was a part of now, and the recruiter, the agent, they were the type of men I would be around from here on out.

I glanced at the recruiter. "Do you ever get used to all of the concrete?"

"Not if I can help it." The recruiter slapped me on the shoulder and smiled for the first time since I had walked into his office. "And don't worry. You become a Ranger, you won't be seeing much concrete."

I nodded once as the agent came out of the building. Glancing at the recruiter, he held his hand out. "Thanks for your help, Staff Sergeant. We'll see you tomorrow."

"Counting on it." The recruiter shook the agent's hand. "Now, if you'll both excuse me, I have a few phone calls to make." He turned to me and offered his hand. "It's been a pleasure meeting you, Scott. I look forward to meeting your wife."

I did not like his last statement, and I did not want to shake his hand, but I did it anyway, even though no one at River Ranch enacted that gesture. "I am counting on you to uphold your word."

The recruiter's expression turned serious. "Of course. Once Agent Morrison gets the paperwork, we'll get everything sorted. See you tomorrow." He walked into the building.

The agent glanced at a four-door vehicle parked in front of us. "Come on, it's late. I'll drive you at least half way." He walked toward the driver side.

I hesitated. Weighing the time it would save me getting back to my woman against the safety of letting the agent know the general location of our cabin, I made a decision. He already knew the general location of where we were, and admittedly, I was curious about being inside a moving vehicle.

The agent paused at his open door. "I promise, I won't come looking for you in the woods." He let out a short chuckle. "Trudging through the Glades definitely isn't on my bucket list."

I made for the vehicle.

The agent nodded and got behind the wheel.

As soon as I was in the passenger seat and had the door closed, I regretted my decision. The space was much more confining than the cabin that first night and the smell was stale with old food and unwashed bodies.

The agent turned the engine over as he pulled a strap across his chest and clicked it into place by his hip. "Where am I taking you?"

Air blew on my face, and I brushed my too-long hair out of my eyes. "Do you know the main road that bisects this one ten kilometers to the south?"

"Yeah, the one that goes west toward Homestead?"

I did not know where Homestead was, but I needed to go west. "Yes. Take that road until it ends at the old county road and you can drop me there."

I would approach the cabin from the north like we did the first time my woman took me there. That way I could check to see if she had returned there before I went to her father's property. Even though I told her I did not want her traveling the woods by herself, I was under no illusion that she would obey. My woman was as stubborn as she was capable.

The agent let out a low whistle. "You walked far today."

"I walk far every day." I had been training my body to be stronger.

"Good for you." He pulled out of the parking lot and a beeping noise came from the dashboard. "You need to buckle your seat belt."

I pulled the strap on my side and mimicked how he had clicked his into place. The beeping stopped, and for a few moments we drove in silence until the agent spoke up.

"Mind if I ask you something?"

"No." He could ask, I just may not answer.

"Why the Army?"

I thought about not answering, about preserving the identity of the one brother on the compound I had respected, but I had already told the agent everything else. I did not see the harm. "One of the brothers on the compound used to be an Army Ranger. I respected him." It was the simplest form of the truth.

The agent stiffened in his seat. "You sure he was a Ranger?"

Mimicking how my woman would raise a shoulder when asked a question she was unsure of, I shrugged. "He shot better than any other brother. He had a stillness about him, was stealth like no other, and he had a peace of mind that was not common amongst the brothers. He was never rash in decision nor temper, and he was intelligent." I glanced at the agent. "He is the one who made me memorize the address of the recruiter when my birth mother passed."

A deep frown creased the agent's forehead. "Blond hair, brown eyes, six feet, walks with a slight limp?"

It was my turn to frown. "Those descriptions fit him, yes."

"Goes by the name Achilles?"

My hand reached for a knife I no longer carried in my pocket. "There is a brother by that name on the compound."

The agent abruptly pulled the vehicle to the side of the road and looked at me. "When was the last time you saw him?"

"The night I was vanquished."

"He was alive?" The agent did not ask the question, he demanded it.

"Yes."

"About thirty-five years old, has a small scar on his cheek?" He pointed to his left cheek bone.

Fear for the one brother who had given me the will to carry on spread. "Why are you asking?"

"His name isn't Achilles. His real name is Lucas John Malach. He was an Army Ranger for a couple years before he was blown up downrange and medically discharged for a leg injury." Staring at me, the agent paused. Then he threw me. "The FBI picked him up the second the ink was dry on his discharge papers from the military. A couple months later, he was sent in undercover to River Ranch. Six weeks later we got one report from him. He communicated that Stephens named him Achilles because of his limp and that he was getting close to him and to stand by. Next communication he would have more information. We never heard from him again. That was fifteen years ago. He's been assumed dead."

Many thoughts clouded my perspective and I looked

out the front windshield of the vehicle. "I do not remember exactly when he came on the compound." I was young and fearful of not completing my assigned duty as the newly minted digger when the old one had passed. "But I think it was shortly before I was five turns around the sun."

"The timing sounds right. How did Malach seem last time you saw him? Was he…." The agent spread his fingers wide and tilted his hand back and forth.

I did not know the gesture, but I understood the question. "He appeared of sound mind."

"Then why the hell would he go off the radar? Was he with a woman?"

"He was with many women. We all were."

"Jesus Christ," the agent muttered, rubbing his hand over his chin. "I have to ask. Did Stephens get to him? Brainwash him?"

I looked the agent square in the eye. "River Stephens gets to everyone." One way or another. "I need to return to my woman."

"Understood." He pulled back on to the road.

The rest of the drive, he did not speak and neither did I.

When the road ended at the old county road, the agent pulled over again. "I'll be at the recruiter's office tomorrow by ten a.m."

I did not have a watch, nor did I know how to tell time, but I knew enough to know that was before the sun was highest in the sky. We would have to leave the cabin early, but it was doable. "My wife and I will be there."

The agent nodded as I got out of the car. "See you tomorrow."

"Until tomorrow." I closed the door and he drove off.

I waited until the vehicle's taillights were mere dots.

Then I tucked the bag of food under my arm, turned toward the open field fronting the edge of the Glades and broke into a sprint.

Chapter
THIRTY-FOUR

Tarquin

SHE WASN'T AT THE CABIN.

Unease mixed with the hunger in my gut and I quickly ate one of the sandwiches and drank the water. Leaving the second sandwich for her on the small table, I grabbed the piece of wood I had finished whittling that morning.

Jagged points in a cascading pattern, it was the image of fire. She had called me her earth. I had called her my fire.

Pocketing the memento I intended to give her, I secured the cabin door behind me and made my way to her father's property. With every pace along the path we had taken this morning, my disquiet grew.

But my unease did not become panic until I cleared the woods at the edge of her father's property and saw a familiar vehicle and two armed men standing in front of the house with weapons at the ready.

Crouching in the shadows, I took the gun from my back waistband and quickly assessed the situation.

All the lights were on in the house.

There were no motorcycles.

Her father had traveled with only two men before.

At a minimum there were the two men, her father and her mother, but the vehicle could hold eight men, ten if needed.

I had fifteen rounds.

My woman had not come back to the cabin, and the men outside pacing had their weapons in front of them.

They were waiting for me.

There was only one option.

Keeping low and to the shadows, moving slow so as not to make too much noise, I got as close as I could. When I dropped to the ground, the scrub brush rustled and one of the men turned toward my direction.

Aiming at my location, the taller man looked through his scope. "You hear that?"

I exhaled.

The shorter man looked in my direction. "It's probably a python. You know how many fucking snakes are out here?"

I pulled the trigger.

"That's not—"

The taller man dropped dead as I sighted on the shorter man.

"Oh shit. *Boss!*" The shorter man fired a shot in my direction.

I pulled the trigger a second time.

The front door flew open, the shorter man dropped dead and Stone Hawkins came out of the house.

"Tarquin Scott." No weapon, Hawkins held up a cell phone. "Your aim precedes you."

I sighted on him. "Where is she?" He had five seconds before I pulled the trigger.

"I think the more important question is this. Do you want to save her?" He moved the cell phone around in front of him. "Or go to jail?"

Fury, instant and consuming filled my veins. "*Where is she?*" I demanded.

Like his daughter, Hawkins shrugged. "She's not looking good, I can tell you that much."

The hysterical woman stumbled out of the front door and lunged for the phone in Hawkins's hand. "She's dying! Give me that. *She's dying.*"

Hawkins held his cell phone up higher as he pushed the hysterical woman out of his way. "Make a decision quick, Scott. Go to jail for killing my men, or save Shaila."

On her knees, the hysterical woman grasped at Hawkins's leg. "Call 911! Give me the phone! She's gonna bleed out!"

Enraged, my weapon aimed, I stepped out of the brush. "I do not care if I go to jail. If you do not want to die in the next two seconds, tell me what you did to my woman."

"I didn't do anything." Hawkins glanced at the hysterical woman. "She did. Pushed her off the porch." He shrugged again. "Apparently you knocked up my daughter, but let's say her mother took care of that problem."

Blinded by fury, I moved.

I did not see the men at the side of the house. I did not hear the safeties on their weapons disengage. I did not listen to the wailing warning from the hysterical woman.

I covered the distance between me and Hawkins and

pressed the barrel of my gun directly against his forehead. "WHERE. IS. SHE?"

Holding his hands up, playing me like a fool, he smiled as the cold metal of two weapons hit each side of my temple. "If you kill me, she dies."

"What do you want?" I ground out.

"You."

My nostrils flaring, adrenaline pounding, I asked what I should have upfront. "Is she alive?" My own life be damned, if she was dead, I was pulling the trigger.

"For now." He lowered his hands. "But not for long if you don't make a decision. I can send this video of you shooting my men to the FBI agent you spoke to today and have a nice chat with him while Shaila bleeds out. Or? You come work for me, join my club and be my Sergeant-at-Arms, and I'll call an ambulance to save her life." He lifted an eyebrow casually. "Your decision."

My mind twisted. "How do you know who I spoke to today?"

He leaned forward as much as my barrel to his forehead would allow. "I know everything that happens in South Florida."

A cry of pain came from inside the house.

I surged forward.

Hawkins's hand hit my chest as other hands grasped my arms.

"Ah, ah, ah," Hawkins warned. "Decision first. Clock's ticking. She's been bleeding for a while now."

"You planned this." My jaw clenched, my muscles locked, rage warred with anxiety for my woman's life.

"Can't take credit for this one. Shaila was stupid enough to come check on her mother. I only seized the opportunity."

"Call 911!" the woman wailed.

"I am not working for you. I am committed to the United States Army. If you do not want to die, let me through."

Hawkins waved his hand dismissively. "Fine, join the Army, get it out of your system. You'll learn tactical warfare anyway, which will only make you more valuable to me. Then you'll come work for me."

"I will not." I glanced over his shoulder. I could not see my woman in the house, but I saw the blood on the floor. "SHAILA!"

Weak, thready and sounding nothing like my woman, her voice drifted out of the house. "Tarquin."

I pressed my gun harder into Hawkins's head. "Move. *Now.*"

A master manipulator, Stone Hawkins dug the last shovel of dirt for my grave. "Come work for me and we'll take down River Stephens together."

"*Tarquin,*" my woman cried.

There was no choice.

There was never a choice.

I dropped my gun. "Make the call."

He did not lower his hand. "Just in case you're thinking you'll be able to back out of our deal after your time in the Army, know this." He waved his phone around and tipped his chin at the men on either side of me. "I've got all the evidence I need to send you to the electric chair. You don't keep your end of the bargain, the FBI gets everything I have on you *and* on Shaila, including where the bodies are buried that you two left here months ago. It won't just be you going down." He leveled me with a look. "Both you and Shaila will be arrested. Do we understand each other?"

I vowed then and there, no matter what, I would not just kill him. I would make him suffer. "Make. THE CALL."

Slow, like he had all the time in the world, Stone Hawkins brought his phone to his ear and smiled. "Bring the ambulance around." He dropped his hand from my chest.

I shoved the bastard out of my way and rushed into the house. "Shaila!"

"Tarquin," her voice even weaker, she barely got my name out.

My gaze frantic, I followed the trail of blood.

When I saw her, the organ in my chest stopped.

I had been a digger.

I had seen death.

I had seen murder.

I had seen more life's blood than any one man should ever see in a lifetime.

But I had never felt it.

Not like this.

My knees gave out, and I dropped my gun as I reached for my woman.

Blood smeared on her cheek, her face ashen, her limbs limp, tears fell from her bloodshot eyes as a giant pool of red lay between her blood-soaked thighs. "I lost him, Tarquin. Our baby, he's dying. Oh my Jesus, he's dying inside me. Tarquin, please, save him. Save his soul."

Rage mixed with fear and I forced words past my suddenly thick tongue. "I am here." Her skin cold, her body shivering, I held her to me, and I lied for the first time in my life. "You will be all right. It will be all right." I had never seen someone lose so much blood and live.

"Candle," she cried. "Light a candle for our baby." She choked. "Save his little soul. Make sure he goes to heaven. Light a candle."

Commotion sounded behind me as two men in uniforms rushed into the house. "Move aside, sir. Let us get to her."

My arms tightened around my woman. "I am not letting her go."

"Candle," she cried harder. "*Candle.*" She sucked in a labored breath and all at once, her body went stiff and her eyes rolled back in her head.

"Move, move, move!" one of the men in uniform shoved me aside as the other took my woman from my arms.

The hysterical woman started screaming. "My baby, my baby! Save my baby!"

The two uniformed men issued commands and spoke words in rapid succession to each other I did not understand as they pressed a device to my woman's chest. *Cardiac arrest, massive hemorrhage, miscarriage, shock.*

My woman's back arced off the ground, the men shouted at each other to be heard over the hysterical female, the machine beeped, and they pressed the device to her chest again.

A voice I did not recognize as my own rumbled from my chest. "What is happening to her?"

Hawkins nodded at the two men who had held guns to my head. "Get him out of here."

"No." I shoved to my feet as my woman's chest arced off the ground again.

"Rip, Link," Hawkins barked. "I said get Scott out of here."

The two men grabbed me as the uniformed men suddenly stopped attending to my woman.

"NO." I fought against the men's hold on me before I yelled at the uniformed men. "Don't stop! Help her!"

The two uniformed men looked at each other, then Hawkins.

Hawkins nodded at his men.

One uniformed man looked at his watch. "T-O-D twenty-one hundred hours—"

The hysterical woman's screams turned to a keening wail that blocked out the uniformed man's words.

I yanked out of the Hawkins's men's grasp and wrapped my hands around the throat of the nearest uniformed man. "FIX HER. *Fucking fix her!*"

Hawkins's hand landed on my shoulder. "Too late."

Fury.

Blinding, breathless, chest constricting, *fury*.

I swung.

My fist hit flesh and I swung again.

Metal hit the back of my neck.

My feet stumbled.

I swung again.

My knuckles contacted with cartilage, the woman's keening abruptly stopped and I kept swinging until I was thrown against the wall, then out the door.

I hit the steps, then I hit the earth.

I was earth.
Men shouted.
My woman had told me I was earth.
Words flew.
I heard none of it.
Too late.
My woman.
Too late.
My woman.
Too late.
My son.
Too.
Late.
I thought I knew rage.
I thought I knew pain.
I shoved to my feet.

"You got two choices," Hawkins yelled. "Nothing's changed. Meet that recruiter tomorrow morning, join the Army and get straightened out, or go to jail and rot."

I did not have two choices.
I had no choice.
I aimed for the woods.
"I will find you," Hawkins warned.
Too late.

Chapter
THIRTY-FIVE

Tarquin

THE HELO'S ENGINE WHINED TO LIFE AND THE BLADES STARTED to thump.

The ink on my new tattoos itched.

The soldier sitting next to me smiled and spoke above the noise. "What's your name?"

I palmed the small piece of wood in my pocket and ignored him as I pulled it out. The carving stained with her blood, the last words my woman begged of me whispered through my mind like a cruel joke.

Candle. Light a candle for our baby. Save his little soul. Make sure he goes to heaven. Light a candle. Candle. Candle.

The soldier leaned forward and looked at the patch above my left breast. "I don't mean your last name."

My woman's blood forever on my hands, I stared at the small wooden flame I had carved for her. Stroking the piece with my thumb, I stroked my rage.

"They're always calling us by our last names." The soldier laughed. "I mean your first name. Mine's Jimmy." He held his hand out.

I looked at his extended hand, but I did not take it. "Candle."

The soldier laughed again. "What?"

"My name is Candle."

Tarquin was dead.

"Candle? Really?" the soldier asked.

I didn't answer. My back and arms sore from this morning's PT, I flexed my biceps that were almost twice the size they were nine months ago.

"Well, okay then. Nice to meet you, Candle. Where you heading?"

I leaned back against the cold metal of the transport. My body conditioned, my training complete, I closed my eyes and silently spelled the seven letter word that had become my mantra. J-U-S-T-I-C-E.

Then, without opening my eyes, I answered the soldier. "War."

I was going to war.

THANK YOU!

Thank you so much for reading HARD JUSTICE, the second book in the Alpha Antihero Series!

To continue the Alpha Antihero Series, and to find out what happens in the exciting conclusion of Candle's story, grab your copy of HARD SIN now!

The complete Alpha Antihero Series!
HARD LIMIT
HARD JUSTICE
HARD SIN

Have you read the Alpha Bodyguard Series!
SCANDALOUS
MERCILESS
RECKLESS
RUTHLESS
FEARLESS
CALLOUS
RELENTLESS
SHAMELESS

Have you read the sexy Alpha Escort Series?
THRUST
ROUGH
GRIND

Have you read the Uncompromising Series?
TALON
NEIL
ANDRÉ
BENNETT
CALLAN

Turn the page for a preview of HARD SIN, the exciting conclusion to Tarquin 'Candle' Scott's story!

Hard
S I N

One breath.

One second.

One moment.

I used to measure my life in single instances. Eight years ago, I thought it was all I needed.

But I didn't escape the most violent cult in the country and survive four tours in the Army because of single moments. Every damn day I woke with air in my lungs, I paid for it. My childhood stolen, my future robbed, my life hijacked, I paid every second of every day for it.

I'd never been free, and I didn't think I ever would be… then a single second changed everything.

*HARD SIN is not a standalone story. It is the third book in the Alpha Antihero Series, and it is the conclusion to Tarquin "Candle" Scott's story.

The Alpha Antihero Series:
HARD LIMIT
HARD JUSTICE
HARD SIN

About the
AUTHOR

Sybil grew up in northern California with her head in a book and her feet in the sand. She now resides in southern Florida, and while she doesn't get to read as much as she likes, she still buries her toes in the sand. If she's not writing or fighting to contain the banana plantation in her backyard, you can find her spending time with her family, and a mischievous miniature boxer.

To find out more about Sybil Bartel or her books, please visit her at:

Website
sybilbartel.com

Facebook page
www.facebook.com/sybilbartelauthor

Book Boyfriend Heroes
www.facebook.com/groups/1065006266850790

Twitter
twitter.com/SybilBartel

BookBub
www.bookbub.com/authors/sybil-bartel

Newsletter:
eepurl.com/bRSE2T

Made in the USA
Columbia, SC
28 January 2020